"Walk," Annie ordered Taylor as she helped him move from the chair he'd been sleeping in to the bed. "Help me."

He was heavier and taller than she remembered, and she nearly buckled as he leaned against her. His feet shuffled next to hers as she did a half-run, half-stumble, pitching forward into a belly landing atop the bed. Trapped beneath him, Annie squirmed.

"If you want me in your bed, there are easier ways," he groaned.

"Let me up, Taylor," she sputtered. "I can't breathe."

As he rolled to his side, his arms went around her, and he swiftly captured her mouth with his. Surprised, Annie allowed his lips to move against hers, warmly, persuasively. The kiss deepened and her tense body softened as he molded her to him. Silk against denim, suppleness against strength—something primitive shimmered between them.

She smelled of wild roses and tasted of honey and wine, a heady sweetness. Taylor felt drunk with sensation as his hands caressed skin as soft and satiny as the gown Annie wore.

Caught off guard, Annie reacted with pleasure, reveling in the touch of the man who'd filled her fantasies. Heat and passion whirled deep inside her, threatening to possess her. If she let him, this man could become an obsession. . . .

WHAT ARE *LOVESWEPT* ROMANCES?

They are stories of true romance and touching emotion. We believe those two very important ingredients are constants in our highly sensual and very believable stories in the *LOVESWEPT* line. Our goal is to give you, the reader, stories of consistently high quality that may sometimes make you laugh, sometimes make you cry, but are always fresh and creative and contain many delightful surprises within their pages.

Most romance fans read an enormous number of books. Those they truly love, they keep. Others may be traded with friends and soon forgotten. We hope that each *LOVESWEPT* romance will be a treasure—a "keeper." We will always try to publish

LOVE STORIES YOU'LL NEVER FORGET
BY AUTHORS YOU'LL ALWAYS REMEMBER

The Editors

Loveswept® 539

Lori Copeland

A Taste of Temptation

BANTAM BOOKS

NEW YORK · TORONTO · LONDON · SYDNEY · AUCKLAND

A TASTE OF TEMPTATION

A Bantam Book / April 1992

If you would be interested in receiving protective vinyl
covers for your Loveswept books, please write to this address
for information:

Loveswept
Bantam Books
P.O. Box 985
Hicksville, NY 11802

ISBN 0-553-44093-4

Published simultaneously in the United States and Canada

Bantam Books are published by Bantam Books, a division
of Bantam Doubleday Dell Publishing Group, Inc. Its trademark, consisting of the words "Bantam Books" and the
portrayal of a rooster, is Registered in U.S. Patent and
Trademark Office and in other countries. Marca Registrada.
Bantam Books, 666 Fifth Avenue, New York, New York 10103.

PRINTED IN THE UNITED STATES OF AMERICA

OPM   0 9 8 7 6 5 4 3 2 1

One

Everyone knew it: Taylor McQuaid played around.

His presence alone made Annie Malone uneasy. She had a gut-level distrust for his type. Of all the men in Colorado Springs, why did she have to get stuck with him? She crossed her arms and faced her doom with a wire whisk in her hand.

Annie knew how to cook. She'd learned the basics at a tender age; while her mother had worked to support the two of them, Annie had kept their apartment clean and prepared their meals throughout her teenage years.

She'd wanted to get the knack of cooking a few international dishes, so she'd recently enrolled in a night class called "Food, the Universal Expression of Love," which would meet twice between college semesters. The title was a bit much in her opinion, but the course description captured her interest: "For the novice and the experienced, prepare gourmet delights from cultures near and far. Create your own masterpiece."

Annie's first night at Ms. LeBeau's College of

Creative Cooking was already headed for disaster. The large group resembled an eighth-grade mixer, with females congregated on one side of the huge professional kitchen, males on the other. Ms. Le-Beau had announced that after reading the bios submitted with the student applications, she had divided the class into pairs by combining each novice with an experienced cook. Peer tutoring, she'd explained, was innovative and productive for everyone. Then Ms. LeBeau had read off her first twosome: Taylor McQuaid and Annie Malone.

New challenges usually fired her enthusiasm, but tonight Annie felt trapped. She pasted a brave smile on her face, but the telltale frown between her brows revealed her disappointment. Out of the corner of her eye she spied Taylor McQuaid.

He stood a head taller than his two buddies, who were leaning against the countertops on either side of him. She glanced at the trio from time to time. The faces of his friends were Hollywood handsome, but she found herself reluctantly deciding that Taylor was even better-looking. It seemed that experience had carved what looked like character into his face. But of course, Annie reminded herself, looks can be deceiving.

His bearing reflected pride and more—a barely concealed arrogance she found annoying. Exasperated, Annie paced around the room, checking out the state-of-the-art equipment.

Before she was aware of it, her imagination conjured up an image of Taylor McQuaid's broad shoulders brushing hers while they worked side by side at their narrow workstation, and an involuntary shiver of excitement raced through her. She sighed in self-reproach, reminding herself that she'd be crammed next to Taylor's colossal ego as well.

Why hadn't she immediately asked to be paired

with someone else? You'd think at twenty-six a woman could speak up for herself, Annie fumed, kneading the back of her neck. Then she conceded that, in all fairness, the man had never done her any harm, so refusing to accept him as a cooking partner would seem both rude and absurd. She couldn't very well bail out now.

Ms. LeBeau's voice rose above the chatter. "Tonight we're cooking Italian—chicken parmigiana. I've included a recipe, but don't ignore your better instincts. This is *not* a class where we must all plod the same culinary path." Her shoulders lifted. "Experiment. Express yourself." Her voice softened. "Remember, the proverbial way to a man's heart. . . ." Laughter rippled through the room.

"This will be," she continued, "a challenge to minds and wits because"—she paused for dramatic effect—"at the end of this two-week course, four of you from this class will be selected to present your original masterpieces at a charity cookoff in Vail. Those winning recipes will be published in *Creative Cuisine* magazine and entered in the national contest. Grand prize: an all-expenses-paid vacation for two to Paris." A murmur of approval circulated among the twenty students. "So . . . create something wonderful. Good luck and *bon appétit!*"

Taylor's eyes casually scanned the faces around the room. He had seen Annie Malone with a group of her friends at a couple of the local Friday-afternoon watering holes, but they weren't acquainted. Something about her had always suggested that she'd been dragged along by her girlfriends against her better judgment. She was good-looking, as he recalled, but her attitude had always seemed vaguely disapproving. He'd met his share of attractive women in his thirty-three years, and he preferred friendly ones.

Through the tangle of people hurrying in all directions, Taylor saw Annie, wire whisk in hand, moving toward him. A flush heightened her ivory complexion, and her shoulder-length chestnut hair, smoothed under in a classic hairdo, accented her heart-shaped face. Wide-set eyes, green as slow-moving streams, were watching him, and her lips full and pouting, wiped all thoughts of chicken parmigiana from his mind.

"You must be Annie. The guys told me to watch for a gorgeous brunette." A smile creased the corners of his mouth as he closed the last few steps, his hand extended. "Taylor McQuaid."

"Ann Malone." She encouraged only her friends to call her Annie. But Taylor's smile didn't falter as his firm clasp swallowed her hand. He's smooth, she thought, very smooth.

"Well"—Taylor glanced at the wire whisk in her left hand—"let's see what we can do with that chicken." They walked to their work area, where Annie picked up the recipe card from the shiny Formica countertop while Taylor sorted through the packaged ingredients assembled for them in a cardboard box.

Annie passed him the card and began unpacking their groceries. "Looks like we have everything we need," she said.

Taylor glanced up from the card. "Do you know how to cook?"

"Don't you?" She kept busy arranging the ingredients out on the counter.

He unbuttoned his oxford shirt at the wrists and began to roll up his sleeves. "That's why I signed up for the course."

"To learn?" She pulled her glance away from his strong tan forearms, took a skillet down from the wrought-iron rack overhead, and set it on the largest burner.

"Do you always do that?"

"What?" Her hands stilled as she glanced up at him.

"Answer a question with a question?"

"Did I?"

He leaned down and looked her directly in the eye, and she forgot to breathe. It startled her to see how close his face was to hers. She could see the pale flecks in his dark-blue eyes. Suddenly her knees felt like water.

In a whisper he said, "You're doing it now."

She glanced away. "Oh, sorry." She tried to take a deep breath but felt restricted, as though a heavy weight were resting on her chest.

"Actually, I'm tired of eating in restaurants all the time. And a two-week course isn't a major commitment." He picked up one of the large white chef's aprons, slipped it over his head, and tied it in the back. "I think I'd enjoy puttering in the kitchen—besides, it gets a little tiresome choosing all your meals in the frozen-food section of the market."

She nodded. Why should a sexy man look even sexier in a chef's apron? she asked herself.

"So we both know I'm the novice; you must be the experienced cook." He handed her the other apron.

She shrugged. "I get by." She slipped the apron over her head, and he reached for the string at her back before she could. She tried to ignore the feel of his fingers slowly working the tie in the small of her back, but a tingling sensation raced up her spine.

"Cooking for one?" His gaze moved over her shoulder to her ringless left hand.

She glanced sideways. *So, Mr. Smooth, it didn't take you long to check me out: single, more than likely available. Well, here's one female who won't give you all the answers.* "Sometimes two," she replied noncommittally, wishing her heartbeat would slow to normal.

"Okay. Since you know more than I do, why don't you divide the tasks and tell me what to do first."

She released a breath she hadn't realized she was holding and began to gather utensils. She'd feel more comfortable being in charge. A small part of her wondered if he knew that and was playing her along.

"Here"—she passed him a low-sided pan— "crush the croutons in there until they look like coarse crumbs."

"Can do," he said easily.

She sprinkled a variety of herbs over the croutons as he crunched them down with a mallet. Taking a raw egg, she rapped it against the rim of a bowl, letting the contents drop inside. With a fork she lightly whipped the egg. Then, stepping around Taylor to the range top, she poured a swish of olive oil into the skillet.

When she bent to adjust the flame, her hip collided with his. "Sorry." She hurriedly straightened, taking a step backward as if she'd been burned—and, indeed, she felt as if she had been.

He smiled at her, all congeniality and warmth. "You'll have to cut out the apologies. This is one of those bump-bottom kitchens." He shrugged. "It's bound to happen again."

Not if I can help it. She took a sidestep and bent the other way to view the flame. "Okay"—she stepped around him—"the crumbs look good." She found it easier to talk about their project. "You can unwrap the chicken breasts."

He was about to do so when she suddenly took them out of his hands. "On second thought, I think I'll just rinse them under a warm tap." She turned to the sink nearby.

"Aren't they clean?"

"You can't be too careful."

"Of what?"

"Salmonella."

"Oh." She could tell he wouldn't have gone to the trouble.

Well, she told herself, who cares what he thinks anyway? After she rinsed each chicken breast, she handed it to him. Their fingers brushed, and she felt as if tiny sparks were flying out from the contact, but she refused to look up.

"Now, we just dip the chicken in the egg like this." She demonstrated with the first one. "And then roll it in the crumbs like so." She set it aside on a plate and stepped to the range to turn down the flame.

She glanced up to see that he was following her lead as instructed. He gestured to the chicken he'd just coated. "Look okay to you?"

"Just fine." She watched him dipping another chicken breast, wondering if she might have him figured all wrong. He seemed harmless enough, except for her treacherous body's reaction to his overwhelmingly virile presence.

Then she remembered seeing Taylor's picture in the society section with one gorgeous woman after another, going here, doing this or that. Rumor had it that he led the local brat pack to all the gala affairs from here to Aspen to L.A. and back.

"You make it look easy," he said, watching her preheat the oven. "I like to cook Italian."

"Say"—he nudged her arm with his knuckles—"you don't happen to know how to fix fettucine Alfredo, do you?"

"Sure—that one's a classic."

"Ahhh, my favorite food." His sigh was appreciative. "I'm in love."

Her heart did a little flip-flop, but her mind

recoiled. "Well, now that you're in this class," she said coolly, "perhaps you can learn to make fettucine Alfredo yourself."

He gazed back at her goodnaturedly. "*Maybe* I can," he replied playfully.

"Why don't you sauté the chicken"—she gestured to the farthest burner—"while I start the sauce."

"Okay." Taylor carefully placed the coated chicken in the sizzling olive oil and began pushing the pieces around the skillet with a spatula. The scent of herbs and a whiff of olive oil rose from the pan. Annie inhaled gratefully: It would be easier to ignore the musky fragrance of his after-shave once the chicken was cooking.

"Hey, McQuaid, you're looking pretty domestic there." A young man with a shiny, swingy haircut walked up and tugged on the back strings of Taylor's chef's apron. "Who's your new girlfriend?"

"My cooking partner, Ann Malone." Taylor gestured with his spatula as he made the introductions. "Nathan Patrari."

The newcomer looked as if he'd stepped off the cover of GQ magazine, and Annie recognized him as one of the men standing with Taylor before class. She nodded as she continued to stir the red sauce.

"Hi," Nathan said lightly. "Wondered if you guys got two packages of cheese by mistake." He cocked his head toward his lanky partner a couple of workstations over. "Wesley's bent out of shape because we didn't get any."

Taylor rested the spatula on the rim of the skillet and moved to the counter. Annie spared a glance at their empty cardboard box, then went on with what she was doing.

"We've only got one package of cheese," Taylor said.

Nathan shrugged. "No sweat, old buddy. I'll check out Ms. LeeeeBeau. The old lady digs me." He strolled nonchalantly in the teacher's direction.

Taylor returned to the stove shaking his head.

"A buddy of yours?" Annie asked casually.

"An acquaintance. We were in the same fraternity in college, and he still buys his cars from me. Patrari's pranks get a little old at times, but he's harmless."

"I've heard about his pranks." Everyone in Colorado Springs could recite the exploits of Nathan Patrari, one of Colorado's notorious ski-slope Casanovas. Along with Taylor McQuaid, naturally.

Taylor lifted the recipe card and glanced at the list of instructions; Annie got the idea that he was ready to change the subject. She busied herself tossing the salad.

Taylor had momentarily wandered off when Annie suddenly smelled an acrid odor, like something charred. Turning to look over her shoulder, she saw telltale smoke rising from the skillet at their workstation.

Smothering a cry, she rushed to the range, grabbing for a tea towel.

"I'll do that." Taylor appeared at her side, inadvertently halting her progress.

"I've got it," she said, pushing him aside without thinking. "Just stay put so that I can get around you." As she pulled the skillet away, the flames licked up and set the edge of the tea towel afire.

Taylor pulled her toward the sink, where he turned on the tap full blast and grabbed the sprayer. With a whoosh of high-pressure water, he doused the tea towel, the contents of the skillet . . . and Annie.

She stood silently, her lips compressed, the rising smoke from the skillet darkening her scowl as she glared at him.

He pried the skillet from her hand, set it in the sink, and began guiltily wiping at the dark smudges on her chin with the clean end of the tea towel.

Continuing to glower at him, she stood motionless while he dabbed at the front of her soaked blouse.

Smiling lamely, Taylor swiped at a wet lock of hair hanging limply across her forehead. He flicked it twice, but it stubbornly dropped back into her eyes. His voice was apologetic as he murmured, "Didn't mean to get you all wet."

"Nice work, McQuaid." Taylor turned to see Patrari grinning at him. Taylor was about to give his side of the story when he noticed the class standing in a hushed ring around their workstation.

Ms. LeBeau parted the gawkers and made her way through. "Everyone back to your own workstations. Everything's under control here."

"Mmm," Patrari mocked as he gazed into the skillet propped in the sink. "McQuaid, you got that blackening technique down pat. You'll wow the babes with this Cajun chicken dish for sure."

"Patrari, get lost."

"Return to your station, Mr. Patrari," Ms. LeBeau interrupted smoothly. Chuckling, Patrari sauntered away. "These mishaps occur more often than you'd think." Ms. LeBeau put one hand on Annie's shoulder and her other on Taylor's, and a warm smile softened the lines in her motherly face. "Now, don't be discouraged."

Annie's gaze circled the work area and stopped at the rangetop, where the gas flames were still dancing on high through the burner grate. "I adjusted the flame myself." She looked perplexed as she glanced at Taylor. "Did you turn it up?"

"I didn't touch it," he said defensively.

"Well"—Annie reached to turn the burner off—"the knob is turned up all the way."

Ms. LeBeau shrugged. "If only the two of you were here," she began gently, "one of you must have accidentally—"

"I have a feeling we have just been the victim of a very unamusing prank," Annie interrupted looking at Taylor. His eyes shifted across the room to Patrari, who smiled broadly and gave them a two-fingered salute.

"Very funny," Taylor muttered.

"It doesn't matter how it happened," Ms. LeBeau said soothingly, "as long as we learn from it." She gestured toward the smoldering skillet in the sink, and her voice lifted in a gust of energy. "Now just pull together like a team, and don't let this . . . er . . . mishap spoil your pleasure."

Annie sighed and moved to the double sink, where she started a mound of suds on one side while she scraped the scorched remnants from the skillet into the other. Taylor leaned back against the counter and watched Ms. LeBeau do what she was reputed to do best—manage people.

"Now," Ms. LeBeau chirruped, "which one of you has the best-equipped kitchen?"

Annie remained silent.

"It has to be her." Taylor gestured toward Annie. "My kitchen utensils consist of a microwave and a can opener."

"And are you free tomorrow evening, Mr. McQuaid?" Ms. LeBeau asked.

The suggestion of a smile played at the corners of Taylor's mouth. "Why, yes, ma'am, I am."

Ms. LeBeau leaned on the counter and looked into Annie's face. "And you, dear, are you free tomorrow evening?"

Annie winced, "No, I'm busy then."

"And the next evening?" Ms. LeBeau continued.

"You know, this course may be short, but it does require homework. You two have to find time to come up with an original recipe for the contest too."

Annie gave the woman an expression intended to discourage her from continuing in this vein. Taylor was behind her, so Annie knew he couldn't see her face.

Ms. LeBeau accepted Annie's silence as a positive answer. "Ah, I can see that you are free that night."

Annie felt cornered. "Yes," she sighed.

"Wonderful. Mr. McQuaid, why don't you pick up some chicken and go to Annie's at, say, six-thirty P.M. day after tomorrow."

"I can do that," Taylor said cheerfully.

"Wonderful." Ms. LeBeau merrily boxed up the rest of the ingredients. "You'll be away from classroom distractions: You'll fix a marvelous dish." She pinched her thumb and fingers together. "Save a little for me to sample, and take time to plan your masterpiece for the contest in Vail. We musn't forget that." She patted Annie's arm. "And most important, you'll get your confidence back."

As Ms. LeBeau began to walk away, Annie pulled her hands from the dishwater and followed her. As they rounded the corner into the next workstation, Annie quickly pulled the teacher aside.

"Ms. Lebeau, I think Mr. McQuaid and I are mismatched."

"Oh?" Ms. LeBeau looked at her blankly. "What do you mean by that exactly?"

Annie was embarrassed. "I'm not criticizing him," she said hastily. "It's just that we're total opposites. He's a jet-setter, and I'm an artist—"

"You are? How interesting." Ms. LeBeau smiled sweetly. "Do you paint?"

"I'm a woodcarver."

"Oh? Where could I see your work, dear?"

Annie knew she was being sidetracked. Whether it was intentional or not, she wasn't entirely sure. "My partner and I have a small gallery, Collectible Carvings."

"Where is that, dear?"

"Pickwick Plaza, the courtyard with the antique shops and the clockworks up on—"

"Oh, I love that area, so much charm. I'll make a note to drop by this week. How *wonderful* to have an artist in our midst."

Annie could see that she was getting nowhere fast. "Please, I don't mean to make a fuss, but if you could reassign Mr. McQuaid and me before our next class, I'd—"

"Actually dear, I can't rearrange partners now," Ms. LeBeau interrupted her. "The others are already working on their dish. I'm sure Mr. McQuaid didn't mean to burn the chicken." She patted Annie's hand. "I'm sure if you'll just give him another chance . . ."

Annie sighed heavily. She was stuck. With a brief nod she accepted her lot and headed back to her station. Taylor was rinsing the last pot and setting it in the drying rack when she rounded the corner.

One look at her face and he guessed the topic of her conversation with Ms. LeBeau. Around them other students were pulling their casseroles from the ovens and admiring their results. After rinsing the last pan, Taylor laid it in the drainer. He wasn't one to push himself on anyone.

As he wiped his hands dry, he looked at Annie evenly. "You don't like me much, do you?"

She was taken aback by his directness. "Why . . . I don't know you."

His dark brows lifted, inviting her to elaborate.

Under his gaze she felt her throat turn dry and her heart begin to hammer. She took a clean tea towel and began drying pans, just so she wouldn't have to look at him. When she couldn't stand the silence, she added, "I hardly know anything about you, actually."

"Well, I'm relieved to know that we didn't sell you a lemon. That happens occasionally, even at my agency."

"Don't worry," Annie assured him dryly. "I'm not one of your luxury sports-car owners."

He watched her face, gauging her mood, listening to what she didn't say. "I see," he said quietly, as though he understood her perfectly.

Something in the way he'd said it annoyed her, or perhaps she felt a tinge of guilt at seeming so judgmental. "Look, I'm not an inverted snob who picks fault with people just because they drive expensive cars."

He shrugged. "Then, I can assume there's something about me that simply turns you off."

I wish. With a jolt she realized that she was more attracted to him than to any man she'd met in a long time. And the longer she talked to him, the more he seemed to wear down her defenses. Annie's glance flicked across the room to his friends and back to him. "Let's just say I don't have much in common with the playboy set."

"The playboy set," he repeated quietly, angling his head to see her eyes more clearly. "Let me guess: sadder but wiser, right? An old boyfriend, rich, probably spoiled, broke your heart."

She shook her head, fighting back the urge to laugh. "Wrong."

She looked sincere, so he believed her, but they both suspected that his guess hadn't missed the mark entirely.

"So, no long-lost love, huh?"

"I don't play with fire, Mr. McQuaid." His glance moved to the scorched tea towel on the counter beside her, and her gaze followed his. This time she couldn't hold back a chuckle. "Or I didn't before I met you."

Two

As Annie feared, a car pulled in the drive at exactly six-thirty Tuesday evening. Peering through her miniblinds, she saw Taylor McQuaid climbing out of his black Porsche. She glanced around to make sure her shoes weren't on the living-room floor, then checked her reflection in the mirror as she listened to his footsteps echo on the wooden stairs outside her second-story apartment. She fluffed her hair back from her face, not wanting to look as if she'd gone to a lot of fuss for this evening. After all, they were only getting together to work on a cooking assignment, nothing more.

She answered the door on his third knock. "Oh, hi. Come in."

His eyes mirrored his approval as his glance skimmed her jade cotton sweater and trim, faded jeans. Only it didn't seem to be the clothes themselves that he was approving of—indeed his gaze made her feel disconcertingly naked. "Is it okay to park in the alley?"

She made her voice sound matter-of-fact. "Sure. Gallery customers park in front, guests in back."

He glanced around the room as he stepped inside, carrying two brown sacks. "This is nice."

"Thanks. Living above one's work has advantages. Some evenings I go downstairs and work on a project I'm excited about. Other times, it's hard to get away from it all."

"Don't I know." He handed her a sack containing a bottle of wine. "I'd like to see your gallery sometime."

She wondered if he was angling for an invitation. "Visitors are always welcome," she said noncommittally, pulling the wine bottle from the sack. "If you'll excuse me, I'll chill this."

He followed her into the kitchen and set the larger sack on the counter. "What's cooking? Smells wonderful." He reached for the handle on the oven door. "May I?"

She nodded.

He pulled the door open and gingerly lifted the casserole lid. "Is this what I think it is?" He looked inside, and his face lighted with a broad grin. "Fettucine Alfredo."

Annie felt her face color. They both knew that making Alfredo sauce from scratch took time and effort, and she didn't want him to think she was knocking herself out for him. "I thought it would round out the chicken parmigiana," she murmured.

"Will it ever."

She smiled in spite of herself. It had been a while since she'd cooked for someone who was so enthusiastic. Her half brother and business partner, Bear, was always appreciative when she cooked for him. But because he'd come to expect good meals at her place, his praise was modest.

She began unloading Taylor's sack. "You brought enough for a regiment."

"We may run into another catastrophe."

She removed the chicken and carried it to the refrigerator. "I think we both know who caused the last one."

"Nathan's quite a kidder. I owe you an apology."

He surprised her. She thought she knew what to expect from him, but remarks like that confused her. Maybe she didn't have him pegged after all. But then, she reminded herself, he seemed to appear on every most-eligible-bachelor list published. In her book, men like that were usually long on charm and short on substance.

"No apology expected. Shall we get started?"

"I think I remember how the first part of the recipe goes," he said.

"Good."

Later, after the chicken parmigiana was assembled and in the oven, Annie turned her attention to the salad. "I don't know what dressing you prefer," she said, bending to read the bottles lining the inside of her refrigerator door.

"That's the only thing I make from scratch," he confessed.

Straightening, she smiled. "You make your own salad dressing?"

"Sure, but it's not very good." His self-deprecating grin scored more points than she wanted to give him.

She cleared a space on the counter and stepped back. "Go to it."

"It's so simple, I'm embarrassed." His smile was truly disarming, she observed.

"Don't be. The simpler, the better."

She watched while he spooned mayonnaise into a plastic bag, followed by a sprinkle of garlic salt and other seasonings. "I never would have thought of the plastic bag."

"I hate to wash dishes," he confessed. "Besides, this way you don't get tomato juice everywhere."

He washed an overripe tomato and held it inside the bag, glancing at Annie to see if she was watching. "I call this the Taylor technique." He closed his fist and crushed the tomato. Juice squirted inside the bag, and he squashed it until it was pulp.

"This technique is unrivaled," she remarked dryly.

Grinning, he drew his hand out of the bag and washed it off. Then, holding the bag closed, he squeezed the bottom of it to mix the ingredients.

"Very interesting," Annie said.

"But the proof is in the tasting." Reaching inside the bag, he captured a dollop of dressing on his finger and held it out for her to taste.

She hesitated. "Oh, I can wait for the salad."

"Come on. I washed my hands." He almost sounded offended.

To refuse would seem rude. Leaning toward him, she became aware of how close her face was to his, and her heartbeat accelerated. Her eyes met his as she hesitantly tasted the dressing on his finger.

"Good?" He brought his finger to his mouth to lick the rest. Her gazed lingered on his mouth a second longer than necessary, but it seemed impossible not to notice how firm and well-formed his lips were. He lifted his eyebrows as if to ask, "Well?"

For a moment she couldn't think of anything appropriate to say.

He inclined his head toward her. "You like?"

"Yes." Her reply sounded breathy, so she cleared her throat and tried again. "Yes, of course. It's very nice."

"Nice?" He looked crushed.

"Delicious," she amended, and wondered why he

made her feel so self-conscious. She took a step backward to feel safer. It had been no big deal licking salad dressing from his finger, she told herself. People lick ice-cream cones every day. But somehow, between the two of them for that instant, she had felt an intimacy. "Perhaps we should enter your salad dressing as our prize-winning recipe." She was talking rapidly. *Don't start rattling,* she told herself. *You always do that when you're nervous.*

"Enter my salad dressing?" He was surprised by the remark. He would have bet his Porsche that she had asked Ms. LeBeau for a change of partners. He wasn't sure why he felt such a sense of relief that she was evidently prepared to see the course through with him.

"I think we can do better than salad dressing," he said modestly. "It's nothing spectacular. We need a dynamite dessert or maybe some great main dish."

"Well, what do you suggest?" Annie put a pan of water on the stove and turned on the burner. While the noodles boiled, they sipped wine, exchanging casual observations about favorite dishes.

Over fettucine Alfredo and chicken parmigiana, they tried to come up with a recipe for the contest that would be both bold and original. As Annie poured coffee, they were still wrestling with the decision.

"I think we've got the hang of the chicken parmigiana," she observed.

"Maybe, but nothing compares with your fettucine." His sigh was pure appreciation as he scraped the last of the noodles from the bowl. The spoon paused in midair as a thought suddenly occurred to him. "Why don't we enter this in the contest?"

She smiled. "I hate to break it to you, but fettucine Alfredo isn't original."

His face registered mock disbelief. "You're kidding."

She shook her head, smiling in spite of herself. After a moment he asked, "Got any more ideas?" She shrugged.

"Oh, sure you do." His attitude was upbeat. "Think about it. What is it you fix when you don't look at a recipe? I mean, I concocted the salad dressing late one night when I discovered I'd run out of Green Goddess. What is it that you just sort of throw together using your favorite ingredients?"

"Favorite ingredients," she mused. "Well, I love cream sauces like the Alfredo. Sometimes I do this thing with sour cream and dry white wine and pour it over chicken."

"Just sour cream and white wine?"

"Well, no, I mix a little of this and a little of that—you know, just the herbs and spices everyone has in their spice racks."

"Ever see a recipe for it?"

She thought about it. "No, it just sort of happens. A little of this, a little of that—actually, I'm not sure what amounts I use." She shrugged again. "I keep adding until it tastes right."

"Is it as good as this?" He pointed toward the fettucine with his fork.

"I guess it depends on your taste preference," she said evasively, not wanting to build him up for what might be a disappointment.

"Come on. This isn't the time to get modest. You're talking to your partner here."

She smiled a little. To her, they seemed an incongruous pair, but his warmth was infectious. "I'll say it's in the same neighborhood, okay?"

"All right, let's fix it."

Why did he make it sound like . . . an intimate activity?

"We just ate," she reminded him, keeping her voice light.

"Hey, we're talking about new inventions here. Do you think Einstein said, 'Not now. We just ate'?"

She shook her head. "You're outrageous." *Not to mention outrageously sexy.* She'd never have pegged him for a devotee of fettucine Alfredo by his lean, muscular physique.

"Listen," he continued, undaunted, "I brought plenty of chicken. You just tell me what else you need, and I'll run down to the market."

"Actually, sour cream was on special last week, so I loaded up on it, and I think I have some scallions. As for white wine"—she looked across the table at the bottle—"there's enough left to do it."

"Need anything else?"

"The rest is in the spice rack."

He rose and started stacking dishes. "Tell me where to start."

She shook her head as she followed him into the kitchen. He had enough enthusiasm for both of them. "I don't imagine you have any trouble selling cars."

He set the dishes on the counter, then picked up a tea towel and began rolling it up as if he were going to flick her with it. "Are you insinuating that I'm a pushy car salesman?"

"No." She didn't want to encourage him, but it was hard to keep from grinning.

"That's better." Flopping the towel over his shoulder, he turned to the sink and began filling it with hot water. "You could have lost your dishwasher, lady. Remember that."

• • •

Annie sautéed green onions and chicken breasts and set them on a warm platter while Taylor finished the dishes. "Now, let's see if I can remember what I put into the sauce."

He watched her pour a little wine from the bottle into the skillet. With a wooden spoon, she loosened the browned drippings and stirred them.

"I'd sure like to beat Patrari and Barlow," Taylor mused, "especially after Nathan's parting shot about us not standing a chance."

"It doesn't matter to me who gets to go to Vail," she said, stirring in a half carton of sour cream, "as long as it's not them."

They sipped wine and added seasoning to the sauce, at intervals, dipping in spoons to sample it.

"Looks too thin, needs more sour cream to give it body," she said, adding a few large dollops. He contributed a squeeze of lemon juice and a dash of nutmeg.

They joked about the ingredients while they added a little of this and a pinch of that. "Needs a bit more wine," he said, pouring some directly from the bottle.

She stemmed the generous flow with a warning hand. "I don't think either of us needs more wine at this point." Her grin was relaxed, and he decided he liked her better when she was like this: good-humored, playful, without her prickly defenses.

He topped off her glass and his. "Good thing, since this is the last of it." He opened the cabinet under the sink and dropped the bottle into the wastebasket.

It occurred to her that he was learning his way around her kitchen and learning his way around her too. She was enjoying his company, perhaps too much, she thought. She wondered if this was the real Taylor McQuaid, or if he was playing a role, one he was smart enough to know she'd accept. She shook her head and dismissed the idea as too paranoid.

He took a spoon and sampled the sauce from the skillet. "Delicious, absolutely delicious. This has got to be our contest entry."

She tasted a spoonful. "Needs more spice."

They added and pinched and dolloped until Annie finally threw up her hands and quit.

"It's close, but it's not perfect."

"What's wrong with it? I think it's great. It's our ticket to Paris, trust me."

She lifted her brows skeptically. "If we can duplicate it."

"We managed it once; we ought to be able to do it again."

She smiled at his logic. "We know what goes into it, but we still don't know the amounts and the sequence."

He shrugged. "We can wing it. Give me a list, and I'll bring the ingredients. You can bring the contents of your spice cabinet. Surely we can duplicate what we did tonight."

"I'm not so sure, Taylor." She lifted her hands, palms up. "I mean, it's easy to feel creative when you're having a good time. It's another thing when you're knee-deep in competition."

"Are you?"

She looked perplexed. "Am I what?"

"Are you having a good time?"

She felt her heart begin to thud against her ribs. Perhaps it was the wine or standing so close to the stove, but she felt herself uncomfortably warm, under his close scrutiny. "Sure," she said quickly, "it's been . . . okay."

He smiled at her reluctance to admit that she enjoyed his company. It dawned on him that he hadn't had this much fun in a long time. He'd been skiing and dancing in a variety of places with a variety of ladies, but he hadn't enjoyed himself nearly as much as he had this evening. For an impulsive instant he considered telling her that, but instinctively he knew she'd believe he was handing her a line.

Looking into his blue eyes, she realized how close they were standing, how low she'd dropped her guard.

"I'd rather go to class with a recipe card in hand." She forced her eyes away to resist the magnetic pull of his gaze. "I prefer to go by a plan."

"Really? I have the feeling you do your best work when you're improvising."

She took a step backward, turning toward the counter. It would be easier to cope if she kept her hands busy. She found herself smoothing plastic wrap over the casserole dish while she tried to gather her thoughts.

How could he know that? Can men read me that easily? Most people, she knew, found it more difficult to figure her out. They chalked up her contradictions to her artist's temperament. But this man—a man so unlike her, a man so unlike any other man she'd known, was guessing things about her she never intended to reveal.

"I don't usually work that way," she lied. "I need to be organized, have goals, stay on track."

"That can work up to a point, but sometimes good things come when you're not expecting them." He smiled. "Sometimes you gotta go with the flow . . . trust your instincts."

"Some people can afford to live that way, taking it as it comes, leaving it when they want." She pressed the casserole dish into his hands. "Some of us have responsibilities." *And dreams,* but she didn't tell him that. "You can have this." She glanced at the dish and took a step toward the door.

That was her signal that it was time to go. For a second he looked down at the dish they'd created together. Minutes ago he would have felt delighted to have it. But now, for some reason, it seemed like only a consolation prize.

Three

There was an undercurrent of excitement in the flurry of activity at Ms. LeBeau's final class. Couples bent close to each other, hovering over their culinary projects. The spirit of competition charged the atmosphere.

Annie tried to appear calm, but inwardly she was a mass of nerves. She was certain their chicken dish would turn out overly bland from too much sour cream, and perhaps they should have added less wine? At the same time she wondered if some of her insecurity didn't stem from the jumble of confused feelings she encountered every time she thought of Taylor McQuaid.

For days she had speculated as to whether he'd offer her a ride to class. There were moments when she'd hoped he wouldn't because she'd convinced herself that she'd be more comfortable if she spent less time in his company. Then there were moments when she felt waves of disappointment at the thought that he might not offer, and worse, never even think of it.

Late in the afternoon he had called the gallery and casually suggested he pick her up since it was on his way. By then she was so frustrated that she found herself making an excuse about needing to drive herself because she had an errand to run afterward. He hadn't tried to change her mind or intrude on her plans after class, and now she wasn't sure how she felt.

As she sautéed the chicken, she told herself that she'd made a wise decision to put some distance between them. She glanced at Taylor, and he glanced away. Tonight he seemed very businesslike—polite, helpful, but not at all solicitous. It occurred to her that he might be avoiding her.

Perhaps he was just wearing his game face tonight. Or maybe the other night was just no big deal. After all, what a comedown it must've been to have dinner and piddle around in the kitchen after he'd dined at the finest restaurants on both coasts and at many of the exclusive out-of-the-way places tucked in between.

She tried to follow the same assembling sequence they'd used the other night, but it was hard to focus when remembered images of his face interrupted her concentration.

"What's wrong?" Taylor whispered when her confusion begin to seep onto her pensive features.

"I don't know—I can't think. Did we use lemon juice or not?"

"We used lemon juice." He took the lemon away from her and squeezed a generous amount into the pan.

"That's too much!"

"No, it's the exact amount we used the other night."

They furtively dipped spoons into their sauce for frequent tastings, shaking their heads with anxiety. Collaborating in whispers about other additions, they plodded on. Everyone around them was carefully following written recipes, confidently and methodically checking their index cards before each step.

"Maybe we need to be soused to do this," Taylor suggested. They *had* had a lot of wine that night.

"How's it going, babe?" a smooth voice goaded behind Annie's ear.

Startled, she jumped and looked around sharply. Leaning over her shoulder was a grinning Nathan Patrari.

"Get lost," she replied without thinking.

Patrari's face registered mock disbelief. He wrinkled his brow and sent Taylor a look that seemed to beg a rebuttal.

"Yeah, Patrari, get lost," Taylor repeated absently, squeezing more lemon juice into the pan.

Knocking his hand away, Annie moved Nathan aside as she reached for the nutmeg.

"Well, this is the thanks I get for taking my time to come over to say hello." Patrari's face was almost a pout.

Taylor lifted the paring knife he'd used to chop the scallions and ran his finger lightly across the blade. "Butt out."

"My, aren't we testy." Patrari's gaze shifted to Annie. "Must be the company you keep."

Annie smiled sweetly over her shoulder into Patrari's eyes. "Afraid you'll lose?"

"Me lose? Funny, sweetheart." Patrari tilted his chin and walked away.

Annie looked at Taylor with a new light of determination in her eyes. "I think it needs more scallions."

"I don't know—wait a minute." Taylor unwrapped a small custard cup with a dab of the chicken and sauce she'd sent home with him. He filled a spoon and fed it to Annie. "What do you taste?"

"Garlic salt."

"Right."

She nodded and added another dash of garlic salt to the mixture. They tasted again from the skillet, then from the custard cup.

Another twenty minutes passed, and their faces were flushed with effort. It was close, but not quite there.

Taylor finally glanced around the room and saw that everyone else had their entries in the oven. "We'd better call it quits and get it cooking."

He held the oven door while she placed the casserole dish on the middle rack. They hurriedly straightened the workstation while sneaking anxious glances at the timer.

The other couples began setting out their creations in serving dishes on a long banquet table. Many of the platters had been artfully dressed with parsley or grapes, others with radish roses or sculpted melon.

"It has to come out now," Taylor muttered when he caught the censorious look Ms. LeBeau was sending in their direction.

Annie gazed through the window of the oven door, watching the sauce just beginning to bubble.

She shook her head. "Not yet.

Taylor panicked when he heard Ms. LeBeau clap her hands to bring a hush. She lifted her hands and motioned for everyone to gather round. "Now," she announced, "there is a number beside each serving dish on the table. I want each of you to take a small sample of each entry on your plate. At the end of the table pick up a scorecard and a pencil. After you've sampled everything, you may go back for more if necessary. Then rank the five dishes you like best. Score your favorite a number one, your second choice a two, and so on. Give your cards to me for tabulating. At the end of the evening I will announce the two winning pairs who will compete in the charity cookoff in Vail next weekend. Hurry now!"

Nodding, Annie motioned for Taylor to remove the chicken just as Ms. LeBeau was taking her place at the head of the line. Annie quickly sprinkled paprika over the still bubbling sauce, and Taylor hurried across the room in long strides, carrying their hot dish, his hands encased in pink oven mitts.

All heads turned to look at the end of the table where Taylor stood looking for an open spot to place his dish.

"Your place is there on the end, Mr. McQuaid," Ms. LeBeau said kindly, pointing toward a small spot.

He set the dish on a potholder and glanced at the number next to it. "Thank you," he murmured. Then in an undertone that only Annie could hear, he added, "I think."

Their number was thirteen.

After an hour of milling around, tasting and tasting again, all the students had made their selections and turned in their cards. Annie and Taylor were sitting side by side when Nathan Patrari ambled over, looking confident and self-satisfied.

"Well, children, how did you like my anise-almond mousse?"

"Interesting," Taylor replied.

"It's *exquisite*," Patrari said in a conspiratorial whisper. "Everyone loved it, and what an original."

"Mmm. It reminds me of the almond mousse

they serve at Couture Cuisine, with just a drop of anise added," Taylor said in a thoughtful tone.

"I don't think it tastes like that at all." Patrari spun on his heel so quickly that his swingy blond haircut swayed like the fringe on a silk lampshade.

When Ms. LeBeau returned to the room, a hush fell. To her surprise, Annie found herself holding her breath. She hadn't thought the outcome would make so much difference to her. After all, she hadn't joined the class to compete but to learn.

"I have the results," Ms. LeBeau announced. "We have two clear-cut winners. Their scores were the highest and, strangely enough, they tied in points. No matter, both pairs are going to Vail. And the winners are," she paused for effect, "Nathan Patrari and Wesley Barlow . . . and Annie Malone and Taylor McQuaid."

There was a round of applause.

"Tell me, Mr. Patrari," Ms. LeBeau began, "what do you and Mr. Barlow call your dessert?"

Patrari stood up proudly. "Well, since two of the secret ingredients are anise and almond, we decided to call it Double-A Mousse."

"How appropriate," Taylor murmured at a volume only Annie could detect.

"And Miss Malone and Mr. McQuaid, what have you named your masterpiece?"

Annie and Taylor exchanged a quick look. They'd never thought of a name, never considered what they would do if they actually won. Taylor heard Annie take a sudden breath. "Well," he began, "we call it Chicken Malone."

Annie's shoulders sagged in relief, and she felt his hand close over hers under the table. It was as if an electric current passed between them, but Annie told herself it was only the excitement of being chosen to compete in Vail.

"How nice," Ms. LeBeau said. "Now, both Miss

Malone and Mr. McQuaid and Mr. Patrari and Mr. Barlow should arrive at the Raphael in Vail next Friday afternoon with their secret recipes and a shopping list of their ingredients. The hotel will then provide the necessary items and space for the preparation of your creations on Saturday. That night your masterpieces will be presented to the editors of *Creative Cuisine*, and your recipes will be accepted for the national contest. Let's all cross our fingers that two of you here tonight will win the grand prize!"

A rousing applause followed.

"All of the recipes from regional winners across the country will be published in the December issue," Ms. LeBeau announced.

Annie's heart leapt. She had always wanted a recipe published in her name. It would be a tribute to her mother. To Annie, in some small measure, having something published under the Malone name would provide a shred of immortality for her mother, who'd had so little in this world and shared it all with Annie.

Strangely enough, Taylor McQuaid had just made that possible.

Four

Taylor pulled up in the alley the following Friday afternoon to drive Annie to Vail. The back door of her gallery opened and she stepped out, overnight bag in hand.

It had seemed easier to wait for him there. Besides, she didn't want to send him any wrong signals: She did *not* want this weekend to seem like a date—or worse, like a romantic tryst.

He opened the passenger door of his low-slung Porsche. "Hop in."

"Thanks." She slid onto the buttery leather seat and inhaled the unmistakable new-car fragrance. After stowing her bag, Taylor started the engine and shifted to first. A deep humming surrounded them as he drove slowly down the narrow alley to the street.

"Here's the information Ms. LeBeau sent me." He passed her an envelope. Across the front were their last names in fancy script.

"McQuaid and Malone," she read aloud.

"Sounds like a law firm," he joked.

Through the open roof a September sun shot gold through his dark hair, and for an instant Annie could see why girls made fools of themselves over him. Not me, she vowed, willing her pulse to stop racing. No way.

At the street Taylor waited for a break in traffic, then merged the car smoothly into traffic. Annie leaned back against the headrest as a breeze whipped through her hair.

"We have to be crazy to enter this contest, you know," she said.

He chuckled. "I don't know about you, but I qualify."

Annie glanced at him. Inside the small cockpit they seemed so close to each other, hardly a hairbreadth away. His size and strength made her feel small and vulnerable. She glanced overhead. A tenacious hangnail moon was rising in a corner of the azure Colorado sky.

"An interesting collection of gadgets," she remarked, gesturing toward the dashboard.

"Anything you'd need, including a computer."

"Never use them," she said.

"Oh?" Their eyes met for an instant. "How do you keep track of your business?"

She shrugged. "I have an old calculator, but most of the time I fly by the seat of my pants."

His eyes leisurely dropped to where she was sitting, and he smiled with undisguised appreciation. "Well, I wouldn't change anything there."

Finding herself more pleased by his admiring tone than she wanted to be, she blushed and said abruptly, "Hadn't you better keep your eyes on the road?"

"If I must." Despite her cool tone, he felt inexplicably drawn to her. Her lips, stubborn yet sensuous, were enough to fire his blood. As he downshifted and took a corner, he wondered how they'd taste.

She was looking at the view and wasn't braced for the curve. Swaying to the left, her arm brushed his. Her breath caught in her throat as she had the sensation of liquid fire racing through her. It wasn't like her to react so disturbingly to the slightest physical contact with a man. Concentrate on the scenery, she told herself.

As they topped the hill, she spotted a sign: TWIN PINES COUNTRY CLUB: PRIVATE, MEMBERS ONLY. Beyond lay neatly manicured putting greens where morning dewdrops glistened like a thousand prisms. That's when she saw them.

"Taylor, pull over!"

"What's wrong?"

"Shhh." She unzipped the large handbag at her feet. "Hurry." Taylor pulled to a stop beside large, padlocked gates.

"What is it?"

"Deer," she whispered. "A doe and her fawn feeding on the fairway. It'll only take me a minute. I've just got to get a few shots."

"Shots? You can't! Hunting season doesn't open for weeks. Are you crazy? We're still inside the city limits," he warned.

"I don't have a gun, for heaven's sake!"

She lifted an expensive-looking camera from her bag and deftly attached a Telephoto lens. Leaning precariously out of the open top, she began focusing. Taylor reached to steady her, his hands firm against her waist.

"Thanks," she whispered reluctantly. Though his grasp let her balance the camera, it did crazy things to her libido.

The doe stopped feeding and eyed the car nervously, glancing frequently at the unconcerned fawn at her heels. "Easy, Mama," Annie murmured. "This won't hurt a bit." The camera clicked softly. The doe looked perplexed as she searched for an escape route. Gingerly she bounded a few steps and looked back. The fawn followed. Behind them on the putting green a flag flapped vigorously in the breeze. "This is going to be great," Annie whispered as she kept snapping. The doe moved to a sagging fence, watching the car all the while. She hopped over and blended into the tall brush. Only her head could be seen, popping up and down as she waited. After a second's hesitation in one bound the fawn disappeared.

"Beautiful!" Annie smiled victoriously as she slid down into her seat. Her eyes were glowing. "Sorry for the interruption, but opportunities like that don't come along every day."

"No problem." Taylor studied her flushed features. Annie was always pretty, but at this moment her enthusiasm transformed her into a beauty. He tried to ignore the strange pull he was beginning to feel every time he looked at her. "I didn't know what you were up to. Are you a photographer too?"

"No, but the pictures I take serve as models for my woodcarvings." Removing the lens, she shrugged. "I could use photos from books and magazines, but it isn't the same. I get more energy—call it inspiration—from the scenes I shoot myself." She stowed the camera and zipped the bag. "I'm gathering wildlife shots for a series I'm doing." Gratitude softened her tone. "Thanks for stopping."

"I really would like to see your work," he said quietly.

"New customers are always welcome," she returned lightly. Glancing up through the open top at the heavy boughs overhead, she seized the opportunity to switch the subject. "Look"—she

pointed to autumn leaves the color of new gold—
"the aspens are so beautiful this time of year."

Her obvious ploy made him smile as he switched
on the ignition. He backed onto the highway and
took off.

After a few miles she leaned back, relaxing a bit.
Annie planned to play it cool this weekend. Taylor
would come away with no mistaken impressions of
her. They were so entirely different. She'd had to
struggle for everything, and he had it all.

Obviously he'd been raised in the lap of luxury,
she thought, glancing at his lap, watching the sun
above the trees splash crazy dapples of shade across
the muscular bulging of his thighs and . . . She
snapped her head away suddenly.

"Something wrong?"

"No!" she replied quickly, hoping he hadn't seen
her staring. "Nothing." Pressing her hand to her
lips, she looked out her window.

"You checking it out?"

"What?" she stammered, glancing at him in
alarm, and then away as suddenly.

"I saw you," he accused.

"No, really." Her heartbeat became frantic; she
felt trapped. How had he seen that one innocent
look?

"Admit it. You were looking."

"It was unintentional," she murmured.

"Let's be honest with each other, Annie."

"Can we drop the subject?" she said shortly, so
embarrassed she wanted to sink through the up-
holstery. "It won't happen again!"

"All right, but I haven't met a woman yet who
wasn't curious."

"What?"

"If you're wondering, speak up," he stated
calmly.

"Look, I've given you the wrong impression."

"No apologies necessary. I understand."

She squirmed in her seat, hardly able to bear his rational tone.

"Come on," he said coaxingly, "admit it. You were so sure I was speeding, you looked over to check it out. Hey, I was only going thirty-five miles an hour. You saw it for yourself on the speedometer."

"Oh. Right." She went limp with relief.

"Some guys get uptight when they think somebody's checking them out, but it doesn't bother me. If I'm driving too fast, say so."

"Thank you," she whispered.

"The last thing I want is a speeding ticket."

"Sure."

"After all, we're partners." He glanced over at her and smiled. "Right?"

"Right."

His brows lifted with concern. "You're looking a little pale. You okay?"

"Just a little edgy." She drew a deep breath, trying to regain her strength. "The competition coming up and all."

"Don't worry. I feel good about this weekend. I think we'll have something to celebrate." His voice was husky and conspiratorial.

"I hope so."

He glanced over again with another heart-stopping smile. "I have a memory for lovely faces." And she had style and polish to boot, he decided. "Haven't I seen you driving a red compact around town?"

She nodded. "It's on its last legs. But, of course, not everyone can afford a Porsche."

"Do I detect a note of sarcasm?"

"I didn't mean to sound petty—sorry."

"No, go ahead. Something about me bothers you. Why don't we get it out in the open."

"Well, pardon me, but I don't understand people

who feel they have to drive macho cars and belong to exclusive clubs."

"Exclusive clubs?" He wondered what was really bothering her. From the moment they'd met, he'd sensed a barely concealed anger below the surface. There were moments he swore he could see resentment churning in her eyes.

"You belong to all the country clubs, right?"

He nodded. "Good for business."

"And the Porsche Club."

"So?"

"Well, isn't it a fact that you can't join that club unless you own a Porsche?"

He shrugged, feeling annoyed. "Frankly I never met anyone without a Porsche who wanted to join. It's a matter of choice."

"And good taste, of course," Annie added.

"Naturally." Amusement tugged the corners of his mouth, and Annie grew irritated when she decided that he was laughing at her.

"Well, it seems snobbish to me when not everyone can afford one."

"Now, that's not exactly true," he stated, shifting into a lower gear. "Take the old nine-fourteens. Some cost less than your compact." She'd like to deny it, but he was the expert. "And *macho* automobiles? Aren't you laying it on a little heavy?"

"Maybe." Annie wished she'd never brought up the subject.

He pulled over, came to a stop, and turned to looked her in the eye. "Annie, I'm not too good to drive something else"—his look was penetrating, personal—"but I'm not fickle." She wanted to break contact, but his gaze held hers. "When I find something I like, I want it." His head suddenly lowered, and her heart pounded when she realized that he intended to kiss her.

Just then a horn blasted, shattering the spell. Taylor glanced into his rearview mirror.

"Hey, McQuaid, get the show on the road." Behind them two men in a yellow convertible were waving. The driver tooted the horn again. "Put your moves on her tonight!"

"Damn!" Taylor muttered, recognizing the intruders.

"Who are they?" Annie glanced at the car behind them.

"Patrari and Barlow—who else? Wouldn't you know Patrari'd be on the road at the same time we are."

"What's his problem?"

"Too much idle time on his hands." Taylor switched on the ignition and pulled back onto the road. "Nathan inherited a pile of money at birth, so he doesn't work. He just spends his time competing in one sport or another. He'll do most anything to win at anything he goes after."

Annie nodded. It sounded familiar, too familiar.

Taylor took to the back roads for a while to avoid traveling the same route as Patrari.

At a high mountain pass he pulled off the road into a rest area so that they could admire the breathtaking view. There were no other cars in sight. They sat for a long moment, sharing the panorama without words.

She sighed. "It is beautiful country, isn't it?"

"Beautiful," he agreed, his gaze moving over her face.

"It's amazing how the mountains still fascinate me. Maybe that's why I've stayed."

Her eyes danced as she glanced up at Taylor, and something inside him turned over. "You're gorgeous when you smile." He hadn't meant to say it aloud, but since he had, he reached out and caressed the petal softness of her throat, resting his thumb where her pulse began to jump.

"Downright ugly when I don't, huh?" she added, hoping to distract him.

"I wouldn't turn you away." A sensuous light crept into his eyes.

"It's getting late." Her smile disappeared like the sun behind a cloud.

Taylor released the breath he'd been holding. She puzzled him. "What do you have against me?" he asked softly.

She looked away and shrugged. "Nothing against you personally. I just don't have much use for playboys. They take what they want and never see what they leave behind." The memory of the shattered expression on her mother's face the day her father had walked out still haunted her. From that day forward, her mother had impressed upon her the fact that money corrupts. Her mother had become convinced that her husband had left her for the easy life that money can provide. After his divorce Annie's father had a fling with a wealthy heiress and had been too busy running through her fortune to spend much time with the child from his first marriage. Eventually he'd married again, fathered and abandoned another child, gone after yet another woman with money. . . .

If Annie had learned anything from those painful years, it was to distrust the wealthy. Somewhere along the line she'd come to associate the good life of the rich with her abandonment and lonely childhood.

The haunted look that came into Annie's eyes startled Taylor. For an instant her eyes were stricken, vulnerable. Part of him wanted to question her; another part wanted to take her into his arms. She wouldn't allow it; he was certain of that.

To keep from touching her, he shifted into reverse. "You're not being fair."

"Perhaps not," she conceded. "By the way, you missed your turn back there."

"Where?"

"You were supposed to turn left."

"Damn!" Why did she have to be so exasperating!

Why was he being so disagreeable anyway? Out of the corner of her eye Annie studied the high planes of his profile. She was sure he'd be perfect for a carving called "Arrogance."

He backed up, then made the turn. The Porsche sped off, pressing the speed limit now.

Talking was pointless. She seemed to draw him in only to shove him an arm's length away. Fine, he thought, countersteering out of a hairpin curve. Two can play that game.

Annie was disgusted with herself. She would have let him kiss her back there. With little effort Taylor could ignite her passion like a spark in dry timber. Nothing was turning out the way it was supposed to.

After miles of silence he finally glanced at her, noting the frown creasing her brow.

Taylor could see the rigid set of her jaw. "Are you seriously worried about winning this contest?" he asked.

"No, I'm fine. Just fine." She hoped it was true.

An hour later Taylor pulled into a service station for gas. Annie disappeared into the ladies' room to repair her makeup.

"Hungry?" he asked when she returned to the car.

"Starved." Her disposition had cooled during long miles over humpbacked roads. She'd decided they had a long weekend ahead of them, and being short with each other would only make it longer.

"Mind if we get something to go?" He slowed as they passed a fast-food drive-in.

"No, that's fine with me."

Taylor pulled up to the outdoor menu board and they studied it for a moment before Taylor pushed the button.

"Good after . . . *crackle, crackle.* Welcome to . . . *crackle, crackle.* May I take . . . order . . . *crackle* . . . please?" crackled the speaker.

"I'll have a cheeseburger and a soft drink," Annie decided.

A voice returned statically. "Burg . . . must . . . pickl . . . ?"

"I'm sorry?"

"Burg . . . must . . . pick, *crackle,* hot apple . . . *crackle* today."

She looked at Taylor blankly. "What?"

"You want pickle and mustard on your burger, and would you like to try a hot apple pie today?"

She leaned over him, calling into the speaker. "No, one cheeseburger, ketchup and mustard only, and a small diet Pepsi."

". . . *crackle, crackle* . . . cheese?"

"Yes, I want cheese on my cheeseburger."

"Must . . . *crackle, crackle,* extra onion . . ."

"Excuse me," she murmured as she leaned over his stomach again.

"Anytime." His breath stirred her hair next to her ear, and she felt the vibration of his heartbeat beneath his shirt. She forced her attention back to the menu.

"A cheeseburger, *no* onion, *no* pickle, mustard and ketchup *only,* and a cola of any kind!"

"Will . . . that . . . *crackle* . . . be . . . ?" the speaker demanded.

"Wait a minute." She glanced at Taylor, their faces inches apart. "What do you want?"

His eyes told her it wasn't on the board.

With a sigh of despair she retreated back to the plush contours of her bucket seat and closed her eyes. Taylor cleared his throat and turned toward the speaker. "Double that order and throw in a large fries."

"Thank you. Pull to the first window please."

Now, the voice was clear as a bell.

Taylor pulled to the first window, paid, then passed the white sacks to Annie. "There's a park across the street," he said. "It might be nice to get out of the car for a few minutes."

"All right." The park looked public enough, and he was right—it would be nice to stretch her legs.

Taylor parked under the shade of a huge oak. Unfolding an old army blanket, he spread it on the ground. She was uneasy when he sat next to her, but the tree trunk provided a common backrest.

"Hmmm, feels good to stretch out." Annie straightened her legs as she leaned back. While they ate in silence, an undercurrent flowed between them. Annie found his overpowering masculinity impossible to ignore. When he offered her some fries, she glanced up at him and couldn't keep from chuckling.

"What's wrong?" he asked.

"You're the first to lean against this tree in a while." She reached with both hands to pull away the gauzy spiderwebs tangled in his hair. "Lean over here." He obediently bent toward her and remained still as she drew her long fingers through his luxuriant dark hair. His warm breath fanned her wispy bangs as she inhaled his fragrance, a hint of citrus and something uniquely his own.

Silence weighed heavily for a moment. "I think I

have you fixed up," she said, trying to sound light.

"Thanks."

They finished the meal in companionable silence. After they stood up to go, Taylor folded the blanket and tucked it under his arm. Glancing up, she discovered that he was watching her.

He flashed her a bone-melting grin. "Why don't you and I call a truce, Annie. I promise I'm not going to make any passes at you this weekend, so you can relax."

She nodded, embarrassed that her feelings were so transparent.

"That's better." Smiling, he held the car door open for her, and she got in, feeling very paranoid and foolish.

"Ah, beautiful Vail," Annie remarked as they drove into what seemed like little Switzerland.

They continued down through the narrow streets, past the charming storefronts. The exquisite little town tucked into a high mountain pocket of Colorado thrived on skiers and tourists.

"Labor Day weekend, and the place is packed," remarked Taylor, slowing in the bumper-to-bumper traffic.

"There it is." Annie pointed to what looked like a small Bavarian castle. Taylor spotted the hotel parking lot and swung into the last spot.

The Raphael had a restrained splendor. Oriental rugs covered imported marble. Crystal chandeliers dangled from lofty ceilings rich with elaborate moldings. Taylor and Annie entered the crowded lobby, their eyes searching for the reservation desk.

"It's across the room," Taylor noted.

A large woman with a suitcase in one hand and

two poodles on a split leash in the other blocked the way.

"Excuse me," Taylor apologized, trying to squeeze around her.

"Young man"—the woman elbowed Taylor's ribs—"can you recommend a good hotel in this town? I'm at my wit's end!" she said with a sigh of exasperation.

"This one's nice," Taylor returned.

"This one's *full.* You'd better have a room here, because there's nothing left for miles!" she said huffily.

"There must be something." Taylor continued to shepherd Annie along.

"Guess again! I had reservations for the girls and me," the woman called after him. Glancing at her well-groomed canines, she sighed. "They've over-booked, and the rooms go to a bunch of fools in some silly cooking contest."

"Those are the breaks," Taylor called back, hurrying toward the reservation desk in the corner.

"Rooms for Taylor and McQuaid, please." Annie and Taylor waited for the reservation clerk to punch the information into her computer.

"I hope the rooms are ready," Annie murmured. "I'm bushed."

"Your room is not quite ready, ma'am. We've had a terrible rush today. Perhaps you'd like to try our Happy Hour across the hall?"

"How long will it be on the room?" Annie persisted.

"Not long. Your reservation is confirmed, but housekeeping is running a little behind."

"Come on, they'll let us know when it's ready." Taylor effectively silenced Annie's protests. She sighed in resignation, and they headed toward the lounge.

The room was inviting with its mellow-wood

walls. Candles glowed on each table, and a long copper-lined bar ran the length of one wall.

"What are you drinking?" Taylor found a table and held out a cushioned chair for her.

"White wine, please."

"It's crowded. I'll take our orders to the bar."

Leaning back in her chair, Annie watched Taylor stride across the room, noting the way heads turned as he passed. It wasn't just his good looks but also his aura of command that made others sit up and take notice. A glow of pride formed on her lips, catching Annie by surprise. He wasn't hers, yet she felt proud of him.

As Taylor threaded his way back to her, he smiled at her, and her heart seemed to perform an involuntary somersault.

"Thank you," she said, as he handed her the glass of wine. For an instant his fingers brushed hers, and their eyes met. She glanced away to sever the charged connection, wondering if he'd felt it too.

If he did, he didn't play upon it. He sat, sipping beer, watching the crowd.

Tracing circles in the condensation on her glass, she tried to think of something witty and personable to say.

"Well, look who's here. Looks like the lovebirds made it after all!" They turned to see Nathan Patrari and Wesley Barlow. "Been here long, Mc-Quaid?"

"No," Taylor returned. "Have you?"

"Not long. We didn't count on seeing you again so soon. Figured you two would be off the road somewhere." His tone was rich with innuendo. "Mind if we join you?" he asked, pulling up a chair.

Taylor took another sip of beer before answering. "You might enjoy a table of your own"—he paused—"across the room." His tone was uncompromising.

"Ah, Taylor, don't be a sorehead. Sorry if we bothered you," Nathan apologized, none too sincerely. He glanced from Taylor to Annie. "Tell you what, we'll leave you two alone tonight." He grinned at Wesley. "We know you've got a big day coming up tomorrow, and you'll need your rest."

"You do that," Taylor said.

"It's done," Nathan called over his shoulder.

"You two enjoy yourselves," Wesley chuckled as they ambled off.

Annie sighed as she leaned against the plush chair, sipping her wine. She was glad to see them go. "I think I'll see if the rooms are ready yet; I'm exhausted."

"It's too soon," Taylor predicted. He knew when the reservation clerk said housekeeping was "running a little behind," it was the kiss of death. "We haven't had dinner. We can order something here if you like."

"Why not?"

After eating a sandwich, Annie felt better. The wine—and Taylor's characteristic charm—had served to relax her. Sipping an Irish coffee as a band played softly across the room, Annie watched the couples dancing on the small floor.

She'd gradually dropped her guard. His interest about her carvings seemed sincere, and Annie had found herself telling him her dreams.

"I know that for me to achieve national recognition in the art world sounds farfetched," she finished, feeling rather foolish. *It's an act,* she reminded herself. *His interest is nothing more than a persuasive act.* After all, Taylor McQuaid *was* a ladies' man.

"You'll make it happen," he said quietly.

"How can you be so sure?" She smiled wryly. "We've only known each other for a short time."

"We've probably spent more hours cooking together than some couples spend in a month of dating." His tone was light.

"Ah, but we're not dating."

"No"—he set his glass on the table—"you've made that clear."

"I'm sorry. It's just that you remind me of someone—that's all."

"Things didn't work out well with that someone," he guessed.

She sighed, knowing she'd been curt. After all, what had Taylor ever done to her? "Not the way I'd hoped," she admitted.

"And how do I resemble him?"

"He was a playboy."

He made a disgusted sound, then caught himself. "Let me guess—he drove a sports car?"

"As a matter of fact"—she paused, unable to keep from smiling a little—"he did."

He nodded. "It figures."

"Men in sports cars pursue women for sport," she stated. "For that reason I don't date the sports-car types. Nothing personal."

"No offense taken."

"Glad we understand each other." She slid her chair back. "That room has to be ready by now, unless they're just building it."

"I think I'll hang around here for a while."

Of course, to check out the women. "Shall we meet for breakfast then?"

"Whatever you say."

"Lobby? Nine o'clock?"

Lifting his glass, he saluted her. "Lobby. Nine o'clock."

Annie signaled a bellboy while she arranged for the room key. "Would you step into the lounge and have Mr. McQuaid get my bags from his car?"

"Yes, ma'am." The bellboy headed for the bar in search of Taylor.

Key in hand, Annie stood before the elevator restlessly punching the button.

"Hold it," a masculine voice called.

Whirling, Annie snapped, "What now?"

"I just wanted to show you the way, ma'am. You shouldn't go up alone." The bellboy offered a conciliatory smile. "Might bring bad luck, you know."

"I've had enough of that," she conceded. He probably needs the tip, Annie thought.

As the old elevator moved with a cadence of its own, they exchanged awkward smiles. "Sorry I snapped at you," she apologized.

"That's okay." The boy grinned. "You have a right to be nervous." He stepped back as the door rolled open.

An odd thing to say, Annie thought. Then she realized he must be talking about the cookoff. Following the bellboy to the end of the hall, she watched as he unlocked the door and swung it open with a flourish. Switching on a small lamp in the entry, he placed her bag in the closet and returned to the doorway with an expectant pause. "Enjoy your stay."

She fished out a couple of bills and gave them to him.

"Have a good evening," he said, practically smirking as he closed the door behind him.

Annie walked in to survey the room, clicking on lamps as she went. It certainly was large, she thought, and lavish. But her mouth fell open when she saw the enormous poster bed, canopied and spread in heavy white satin. In fact, the entire room was done in white: damask print on the walls, brocade at the tall window, and silk on the two small chairs that flanked a marble fireplace already ablaze, gilded swans . . .

There must be some mistake. He'd brought her to the wrong room.

She moved to the nightstand and lifted the receiver on an ornate French telephone.

"This is Annie Malone in room eight-twenty-four. This looks like a"—she paused—*"bridal suite."*

Five

"Why—er—yes, it is the bridal suite, Mrs. Mc-Quaid. We checked the bubble bath a few minutes ago, and it was the precise temperature requested."

"Requested by whom?" she demanded.

"Why, by the man who made the arrangements. The instructions were precise," he continued briskly, "and we appreciated receiving them in advance. I hope everything meets your approval."

"It does not." She was trembling with anger now. How dare Taylor McQuaid try something like this on her!

"I apologize, ma'am." The clerk's voice registered surprise. "How may we make you comfortable?"

"Is this room registered to Annie Malone?"

"Let me check. There are two names: your married name, McQuaid, and your maiden name also, to avoid any misunderstanding."

"There's been a misunderstanding, all right. I want to be moved to another room immediately!"

"We'll be happy to prepare the room again to suit your request."

"The only way you can suit my request is to get me another room, which I will occupy by myself!" Annie sputtered.

"I understand your request, Mrs. McQuaid, but—"

"I am not Mrs. McQuaid! I am Annie Malone. Taylor McQuaid is not my husband!"

"I don't think that's any of my business, actually," he said. His patronizing tone began to jangle Annie's nerves. "The problem is that we have no other rooms available at this time. We're completely full."

Annie remembered the disgruntled poodle owner. "Look," she said, growing desperate, "I could trade rooms with somebody."

"I'm sorry, ma'am. That's not possible."

"You won't be paid for this room," she threatened.

"The room was paid for in advance."

Slamming the receiver into its gold cradle, she sat down for a moment. "If McQuaid thinks he's spending the night in this room," she vowed, "he has another think coming."

A loud knock rapped twice. "And it will be my pleasure to tell him where he can go!" Annie stood, crossing to the door in angry strides. She jerked the door open. "McQuaid, you self-serving . . ."

Her words hung in midair as a porter handed her a large basket laden with fruit. "Compliments of the management."

"Thank you." The words spilled out from habit. She took the basket and started to close the door.

"And your bag, ma'am." The boy slipped in and quickly set her bag inside before turning on his heel and heading away. He hadn't even waited for a tip. Annie surmised that at least the staff was aware of her displeasure and seemed to be trying to tiptoe around her.

Setting the basket of fruit on the table, she glanced at the expanse of snowy satin atop the honeymoon bed. If he thinks his little charade will provide him a night of sporting pleasure, he's very sadly mistaken, she thought.

But a vision of Taylor and herself tangled beneath the downy comforter invaded her thoughts, and in frustrated rage she picked up the basket and hurled it, bouncing fruit in all directions.

Unable to remain still, she paced. But the huge bed dominated the room and her imagination. Moving to the bathroom, she covered her mouth with her hand as she stifled a frustrated scream. For an instant the room seemed filled with people. Then she noticed the walls lined with mirrors, reflecting the light of a dozen candles clustered at the corner of a huge bubble-filled tub for two. Two thick towels lay conveniently at the edge. "I have to hand it to you, Taylor, you've thought of everything."

Another brisk knock sounded at the door. "What now, the Trojan horse?" she muttered, her fingers clamping the doorknob as she yanked it.

Again she saw the uncomfortable expression of the porter. "Room service, ma'am."

"Oh, how nice. What have we here?"

The porter swallowed nervously and glanced at a ticket on the cart. "Champagne and caviar to the honeymoon suite."

"From the management?" Annie asked tersely.

"From Mr. McQuaid, ma'am."

"By all means, bring it in. That Mr. McQuaid thinks of everything, doesn't he?" she said sweetly, swinging the door wide. The boy pushed the cart inside and hurried out, again without pausing for a tip.

Annie began pacing, circling the cart like a caged animal. All day Taylor had assumed they'd frolic the night away in this playground for two.

Her face burned with shame as she remembered laughing with him, confiding in him, actually warming to him! "What an idiot I am!"

She heard a key turn the lock, and she froze in her steps, her heart hammering painfully. The door swung open, and Taylor backed inside, toting his luggage.

Turning, he paused, startled. "What are you doing here?"

"Skip the act. It won't work. The honeymoon is over."

He stared at her vacantly. "What are you talking about?"

"Get out of my room."

"*Your* room?" He held his key up, reading the number again.

"Oh, really." She brushed past him, disgusted at how far the man would go.

Taylor dropped his suitcase and walked past her to pick up the phone.

Annie followed on his heels. "Explain why the honeymoon suite is registered in our names as husband and wife."

Taylor stoically dialed the front desk. "It's obviously a mistake."

"My sentiments exactly," Annie said coldly. "*Your* mistake."

"Now, wait just a minute," he said. "I had nothing to do with this."

"Then, how did it happen?"

Meeting her gaze evenly, he said just as coolly, "How do I know that *you* didn't arrange this?"

"Me? That's ludicrous." She picked up the ticket from the champagne cart and thrust it at him.

Taylor took it from her fingers, reading his signature. "I didn't sign for that."

"Of course not."

The reservation clerk came on the line, and

Taylor received the same message—the room was registered to McQuaid and Malone, some sort of wedding nonsense, and no other rooms available.

"There's got to be an explanation for this," he said soothingly as he hung up the phone. But damned if he knew what it was.

"I'm sure there is—perhaps a small error in your judgment?"

"Look," he said heatedly, "I don't resort to cheap tricks to get a woman into my bed." His gaze moved around the room. "And a honeymoon suite?" He shook his head. "Definitely not my style."

"Just leave," she repeated.

Picking up his bags, he paused. "Boy, you're sure of yourself, aren't you?"

"What's that supposed to mean?"

"It means Ms. Malone, that I don't recall even *hinting* that I was attracted to you. You're so damn convinced that I'm after you, your imagination is working overtime."

Picking up a kiwi lying on the floor, she flung it at him.

Green goo splattered against the molding as the door closed behind him.

As dawn broke over sleepy Vail, Annie opened her eyes and struggled to focus on the ivory canopy overhead. She stretched and yawned before scanning the unbroken acres of satin next to her. She was alone.

Then, propping herself up on her elbows, she saw Taylor sprawled in a wooden armchair, his feet thrown atop its mate nearby. His knuckles grazed the thick carpet while his neck twisted restlessly against the unyielding straight back. He pitched to and fro, vainly searching for soft contours.

She suddenly felt her resolve weakening. Since it was Labor Day weekend, she reasoned, there were no vacancies. During the night Taylor must have come back, but at least he'd had the decency not to invade her bed. A shadow of doubt crept into her mind. What if this mess *hadn't* been his doing?

Annie slid from the cozy warmth, denying herself an instant to contemplate the impulse that drove her to his side. Briskly she shook him. When he didn't respond, she stepped to the chair opposite him and pulled it back abruptly. His feet hit the floor with a crash as his torso bolted upright. "What the—"

"Shhh," she interrupted, shoving her shoulder against his side. She pulled his arm across her shoulders and urged him to his feet. He was heavier and taller than she'd remembered, and she nearly buckled as he leaned against her. "Walk," she ordered him, jabbing defensively with her elbow. They'd topple soon if he didn't support himself.

His feet shuffled next to hers as she did a half-run, half-stumble, pitching forward into a belly landing atop the bed. Trapped beneath his weight, Annie squirmed.

"If you want me in your bed, there are easier ways," he groaned.

"I'll bet," she sputtered. "Let me up. I can't breathe!"

As he rolled to his side, his arms went around her, and he swiftly captured her mouth with his. Surprised, Annie allowed his lips to move against hers warmly, persuasively. The kiss deepened as her lips parted before his plundering tongue, and her tense body softened as he molded her to him. Silk against denim, suppleness against strength— something primitive shimmered between them.

She smelled of wild roses, conjuring images of undiscovered delights. Her taste was a heady sweetness, all honey and wine. And he felt drunk with sensations as his wide-spread hands traveled over fabric nearly as luxurious as the skin beneath it.

Caught off guard, she shed her usual inhibitions and responded instinctively. Here was the excitement she'd always denied herself, she realized, as his touch sent shivers racing over the hills and valleys of her body. She reveled in the strength of his shoulders under her hands. Moving up his neck, her fingers played over his face, tracing, molding, memorizing.

Heat and passion whirled deep inside her, threatening to possess her. If she let him, this man could become an obsession. Like a fog creeping upstream at twilight, fear crept into her limbs till it reached her heart.

Twisting out of his arms, she rolled to the edge of the bed. He reached for her too late. "Why?" he asked, a look of disbelief creasing his forehead.

"I didn't mean for this to happen." Her voice was a hoarse whisper.

"But you dragged me over here." He couldn't believe his luck when she'd come to him, nor again when it reversed and she deserted him. Desire had touched her too. Of that he was certain. "Why, Annie?"

"I felt sorry for you." She backed away, sensing danger.

"Sorry for me?" His jaw dropped. "You didn't kiss me like that because you felt *sorry* for me."

She backed halfway across the room. "I moved you to the bed because I knew you were uncomfortable."

Now, he thought, they were getting somewhere.

"Then come back, because I'm feeling uncomfortable without you."

His eyes coaxed and cajoled, and Annie was tempted to take that first step but restrained herself. "No," she insisted, wrapping her arms around herself.

"Annie . . ." His voice was a caress, sweetly intimate.

"Look," she interrupted, "I'm going to change and go downstairs. I'll have the desk ring you about half an hour before we're needed in the kitchen." Before her resolve disappeared, Annie grabbed her suitcase and locked the bathroom door behind her. She took deep breaths to ease her trembling before she showered and dressed in record time.

As she slipped back into the bedroom on her way out, her traitorous glance found him lying flat on his back, one arm resting across his forehead. The sight of him tugged at her, but she scurried out the door and down the hall.

By the time the elevator doors closed behind her, she had made up her mind. She marched to the front desk, gave her bag to the clerk, and found the manager. Once inside his office, she quietly explained that an error in booking had humiliated her. And while she'd rather not bring this unfortunate situation to the attention of the hotel president, she would unless they examined the paperwork together to determine how this could have happened. Reluctantly the manager agreed to open his records.

Besides the reservations for the cookoff contestants, the hotel had received a set of instructions requesting a honeymoon suite for a Mr. and Mrs. McQuaid. Payment was separate, by credit card. Annie released a sigh of disappointment: The hotel was not at fault.

There was one other possibility. She requested a check on the credit card number. While the manager held the phone, Annie held her breath. She released a long sigh when the information came through. The number did *not* belong to Taylor McQuaid; it was Nathan Patrari's.

Nathan Patrari, the joker in the yellow convertible. His mocking smile flashed through her mind. She could hear his parting shot from the night before, something about leaving them alone. He'd left them alone all right, in the honeymoon suite.

No, the manager assured her, Patrari wasn't registered in his hotel. At least not under his own name, Annie surmised. After thanking the man, she headed briskly for the coffee shop.

A prank. The honeymoon suite had been another of Patrari's childish pranks. But why? she wondered. According to Taylor, winning was all that mattered to Nathan. Would he really pull such a stunt to distract them to gain advantage? Of course, she concluded, sliding into a booth. Why not? Nathan seemed short on scruples, long on cash.

It was just the sort of thing her father would've done on a lark. They were cut from the same cloth, she decided, as she turned over her cup and watched the waitress pour coffee. Or were they? Was Taylor like his buddies? Her heart insisted that he wasn't. Her mind insisted that it didn't matter—she would never see him after the cookoff anyway.

He was trouble, even more than she'd imagined. Those moments in his arms had proven it; he could turn her world upside down. But she would never let that happen. She had goals, a future she'd worked for, and she wasn't about to throw that away now.

The waitress took her order for eggs and orange juice. While she sipped her coffee, Annie weighed her options. Dropping out of the cookoff was the safest thing. She could cut and run, catch a ride back to Colorado Springs, and never see Taylor again. Safe and smart—but cowardly too, she concluded.

Her breakfast arrived, and as she spread her toast with jam, Annie thought about Nathan Patrari. If she quit now, Taylor would be out of it, too, and Nathan's chance for victory improved, just as he'd planned.

Well, no way, she thought, holding her knife in midair. Why hand him an easy triumph? Nathan would have to work for this trophy.

Checking her watch, she finished breakfast quickly. She'd made her decision. She dropped a tip, paid the check, and hurried to the courtesy phone.

She punched in the room number and counted five rings. "What?" demanded a masculine voice irritably.

"Taylor?"

"What?" he asked groggily.

"Wake up! Time to hit the kitchen."

"Annie?"

"In the flesh," she said lightly, trying to coax him into a better mood. "What do you like for breakfast? I'll have it waiting for you in the coffee shop."

"Surprise me." His voice held more than a hint of irony.

"Can do," she said.

"Don't I know it." He rubbed his face. "I'll need fifteen minutes."

"You can have twenty."

As he stepped into the coffee shop exactly eighteen minutes later, Annie's pulse quickened. His eyes scanned the room, then widened momentarily when they met hers. His presence was disturbing. Watching him settle into the chair across her table, she inhaled his clean, masculine scent. His hair was damp just above the collar of his yellow polo shirt, and his tanned face was clean-shaven. Only his eyes revealed the strain.

Annie felt a dart of remorse for her share of his discomfort. She waved it aside as she signaled the waitress. Plates of steaming ham, eggs, biscuits, and gravy were placed before him. All the while his eyes studied hers, as if searching for her motive, probing to understand what made her tick. She grew uncomfortable under his scrutiny.

"They call it the mountain man's breakfast." She gestured toward the plates in front of him. "I thought it suited you." Her attempt to break his gaze failed. Nervously she licked her lips as his gaze sharpened. "It's not polite to stare," she said, trying to sound matter-of-fact.

He shook his head. How could he keep from staring? Thoughts of her had haunted him for the past twenty-four hours. And she seemed more alluring every moment. Bewitched. That was what he was. Maybe when this damn cookoff was over, he would forget the way she tasted, the way her scent surrounded him, sweet and mysterious. Then again, he didn't figure he'd be so lucky.

"I suppose there's a reason for"—he paused—"all this attention." He could fight frustration with sarcasm.

His mockery stung. But what had she expected? Didn't spoiled playboys always pout when they didn't get what they wanted? "All this attention, as you call it, is to put you back in shape. We have a cookoff to win."

"You never fail to surprise me, Ms. Malone. I thought you'd drop out about now." Annie's eyes followed as he slowly placed a wedge of ham on his tongue.

"I'm no quitter, Mr. McQuaid."

His dark eyebrows rose sharply, effectively conveying his doubts about that. Her fingers tightened on her coffee mug. Time to enlighten him. "You might like to know who booked our blissful honeymoon," she said, watching his back straighten.

"Who?" His eyes narrowed.

"The room was charged to Nathan Patrari's credit card."

"Why, that son of a—"

"Calling him names won't help," she interrupted. "I've already tried all the ones I know and a few creative combinations."

The corners of his mouth twitched as he watched her work herself into a temper. "No, I don't suppose that will pay him back."

"But I know what will," she confided in a conspiratorial tone.

"Oh?" He enjoyed watching her eyes light up. Such gorgeous green eyes. He liked to see them sparkle with outrage and darken with passion.

"We could win the cookoff!" She gave a vigorous nod, and her hair swung forward and brushed her glowing cheeks. "Surpassing him there would be the best kind of revenge."

"That'd fix him, all right," he agreed. "That and a swift kick."

"Nothing can compare to grabbing the victory he wants."

Taylor ladled cream gravy over a biscuit. "Nathan will be counting on us to pull out."

"Then, let's win." Annie extended her hand to

seal the deal with a shake. Taylor glanced up and hesitated for a few seconds, acknowledging to himself that if he went along with her now, he was doomed. She affected him as no other woman had.

"Agreed." Solemnly they shook hands. His grasp was firm and brief, but Annie felt an electric charge racing up her arm.

Taylor checked his watch. "We'd better get with it."

Nodding her agreement, she downed the rest of her coffee and rose.

They found information packets in the lobby. Annie scanned the sheet. "Our appointment in the kitchen is at ten o'clock," she said. "I don't know what will be expected of us."

"It's tough to negotiate when you don't understand the terms." His eyes held hers, and she knew he was talking about more than the cookoff.

Better if he never understands me, she thought. "We just have to finish this event." And finish with each other, she reminded herself. He stood near, his breath touching her face as he watched her heartbeat pulse in the hollow of her throat.

"Aren't you forgetting something?" His voice sounded lazy, but the undercurrent was insistent.

"No." Her answer came too quickly, too defensively. He lifted one brow, and her face flushed. Gone was their easy camaraderie at breakfast. Again, she was uneasy.

In his gaze was a familiarity, an intimacy, that made her stomach knot. He wanted her. It was in his eyes; he was making no attempt to hide it. And she knew to the depths of her soul that he saw past her hasty defenses, that he knew she wanted him too.

"We're going to be winners." His tone was confident.

"The cookoff," she confirmed.

"That too."

She spun away. She could feel him staring at her back, but it was easier, easier than staring into those blue eyes that seduced her while they mocked her.

"Stay alert," he whispered close to her ear, stirring her senses. "One mistake and we're in trouble."

"Then don't distract me," she warned, trying to concentrate on the page in her hand. "There will be two groups scheduled in the kitchen: one in the morning and one in the afternoon. We're in the morning."

"And so is Nathan," he added, glancing at the list over her shoulder. Taylor scanned the parking lot. "No sign of Mr. Patrari."

"He'll show," Annie said with a resigned sigh.

As they turned to leave, a familiar yellow convertible whipped into the parking lot. "And right on time," Taylor muttered between his teeth.

"We're due in the kitchen," said Annie, taking Taylor by the forearm.

Taylor nodded reluctantly, and they headed toward the elevators.

The morning passed quickly as cooking absorbed their constant attention. Patrari was at a workstation across the huge professional kitchen, so they rarely caught a glimpse of him.

Annie tasted the sauce one final time. "Not bad, McQuaid."

He liked the way she'd said his name just then. Teamwork, he thought to himself. Perhaps a little more teamwork, and she'd get that chip off her shoulder.

"All thanks to you," he said sincerely.

She turned her head and looked at him. At that moment Taylor didn't seem like Nathan Patrari at all; he wasn't greedy for recognition. He was generous and eager to share the credit.

Against her will, she felt the wall between them crumble a little more.

Six

Delicious aromas mingled in the kitchen of the Raphael while various pairs of cookoff contestants carefully assembled the dishes they hoped would win. Annie and Taylor glanced up when Nathan Patrari proudly carried his mousse to the two attendants standing guard at the walk-in refrigeration room. They watched while the attendants, wearing chef whites, labeled Patrari's elaborate mold before taking it inside to a refrigerated compartment. After one attendant closed the door to the cooling room, the other spun the lock. Annie breathed an audible sigh of relief as Patrari and Barlow strode out of the kitchen.

After numerous corrections, additions, and countless tastings, Annie and Taylor finished assembling their Chicken Malone. They decided to wait until an hour before serving to place it in the oven. The chef attendants labeled their dish and placed it in a refrigerated compartment.

Annie glanced anxiously up at Taylor as they headed toward the coffee shop and whispered,

"You know, we still don't have this recipe figured out."

He shook his head. "Well, we know what goes in it."

"But the proportions and the sequence of instructions—we have to get that down pat before we can turn in a recipe to the committee. After all, the winning recipe is going to be published nationwide in *Creative Cuisine.*"

He selected a booth and slid onto a seat opposite her. "We'll just write down the ingredients and approximate the amounts."

Annie looked at him in disbelief. "Surely, you're not serious?"

"Who's to know?" He turned over a cup, and the waitress who poured his coffee smiled down at him.

The woman filled Annie's cup and bestowed another smile on Taylor. "If there's anything else I can do for you," the waitress said to him, "just let me know." Annie felt an irrational proprietary urge toward Taylor and had to restrain herself from grimacing at the overly friendly waitress.

After the woman walked away, Taylor continued, "Do people really follow recipes to the letter anyway? Hey, if I don't happen to have an ingredient on hand, I leave it out."

Annie couldn't believe what she was hearing. "And has that worked out for you?"

"Well," he said a little evasively, "not always."

"That might be all right for an experienced cook, but not necessarily for a beginner." Annie squared her shoulders. "Besides, I'm not attaching my name to something that could turn into a blueprint for disaster."

"Hey, it might not turn out tasting as good as *we* know it can, but whatever somebody does with those ingredients ought to taste okay."

"Okay?" She sat up straight. "*Okay* isn't good enough to be Chicken Malone."

Taylor looked at her and shook his head. She sounded so righteous sometimes. "Well, as far as I'm concerned, *okay* is good enough to be called Chicken McQuaid."

She sent him an icy stare. "You said we'd call it Chicken Malone. Are you going back on your word now?"

His eyes widened. "What's the big deal? Does it really *matter* what we call it?"

She couldn't disguise her disappointment. "Believe me, it matters." She admired his grace when he'd named their dish Chicken Malone. Now she was discovering that he had not deferred to her out of magnanimity—rather the name simply wasn't important to him.

He was accustomed to negotiating with people who got testy at times, but when her voice turned condescending, his patience seemed to disappear quickly. He was on the verge of walking out on her until he saw her eyes cloud with hurt. He couldn't leave her like that.

"Look," he began in a conciliatory tone, "one thing at a time. Let's take care of the banquet this evening. We can worry about the recipe later."

"The banquet." She nodded. "It starts at seven with a reception, as I recall."

They still had only one room—the bridal suite. The hotel had been unable to provide them with another room. He sensed her tension and guessed its cause. "You can use the room first. Take all the time you need. It won't take me long to get ready."

"Okay." His suggestion seemed fair, but it didn't broach the subject of sleeping arrangements for the night. Well, she thought, looking into the coffee she'd hardly touched, one thing at a time. First, they'd get through the banquet. Then they could negotiate who slept where. She glanced at her watch. She was exhausted. What she'd like more than anything was to lie down awhile before she showered.

"I could use the room, say, around four?" he suggested. "That'll give me time for a nap and a change. We could meet in the lobby at seven."

She nodded. "Okay." When she started to slide out of the booth, he raised his hand. "Whoa, how about lunch?"

She shook her head. "I don't think so. I'm more tired than hungry."

"We have a long evening ahead of us," he said evenly. "You want to faint and fall down in front of everybody."

She thought for a moment. Of course, people like him were always aware of appearances. He didn't want her to embarrass him in public.

"Sure, lunch is fine," she agreed.

He signaled for the waitress.

Annie ordered a sandwich and a cup of soup. After she'd eaten about half her meal, her eyes were feeling heavy. She excused herself and headed for the room.

As she walked through the door, the vision of clouds of ivory fabric everywhere rocked her again, like an aftershock—the bridal suite. She'd been so busy that morning that she'd almost forgotten about the room. Her gaze moved to the window, where long silk draperies pooled atop the snowy carpet like the lavish train of a wedding dress.

For a brief moment she felt a stab of disappointment that her stay here was all a hoax. Then she gave herself a shake. She must be more tired than she'd thought. Why should she feel disappointed? She didn't want to get married.

She took a quick shower and stretched out atop

the bed. If she could just rest her eyes for a few minutes . . .

She awakened with a start when she heard a key turn in the lock. The late-afternoon rays diffused by the draperies bathed the room with a soft orange glow. She sat up and struggled to focus on the shadowy form moving into the room.

"I didn't mean to startle you." Taylor stood at the foot of the bed. "I thought you'd be—"

"What time is it?" she cut in, even as she looked at the lighted dial on the nightstand. "Oh, no," she groaned, "four-thirty. It was your turn a half hour ago." With a sinking sensation she realized she should have arranged for a wake-up call, just in case.

"No problem. There's an errand I can run. I could be back in, say—"

"I'll be out of here in half an hour or less," she interrupted. "I'm sorry, Taylor, really."

He waved away her apology and closed the door behind him.

She sprang from the bed and dashed to the closet.

A half hour later she was dressed and heading down the hall. She'd got ready in record time, for a formal evening, that is. She pressed the elevator button and then touched the back of her hair to be sure that the French twist was still secure.

The elevator doors rolled open, and Taylor paused inside for a moment, staring at her. When the doors began to close automatically, they both lunged, reaching out to stop them. Taylor's hand closed over hers.

He stepped out, slowly releasing her hand. With a warm smile of appreciation he looked her up and down. "You look lovely."

Her cheeks warmed. She'd tried to tell herself that she'd selected the new black cocktail dress for the banquet, but every dress that she'd tried on last week she'd judged on the basis of what she thought he'd like. His approval delighted her even as she wished it weren't so important to her. "Thanks," she murmured graciously.

"For you." He held out a small white box.

Annie's eyes widened in surprise. Through the cellophane window she could see a corsage. He opened the box and lifted out an exquisite, fragrant white gardenia. "I found a florist in Vail Village."

"Taylor . . . how thoughtful." She was truly touched.

Shrugging as if such a tribute was only her due, he held the corsage up to her dress and raised his brows. "Here okay?"

She nodded automatically, figuring he'd had more experience with this sort of thing than she. "I suppose." She felt a bit flustered as he deftly slipped two fingers inside the neckline of her dress and wove the stick pin through the fabric and the corsage. Nothing in his face or his touch indicated that his actions were intended for more than pinning on the gardenia, but as his breath touched the wispy curl above her ear, her heart sped up to double time.

"I still don't know why you did this." She felt dismayed that her voice sounded so breathless.

He shrugged nonchalantly. "When you win that trophy, they'll take pictures. Flowers always add a little something."

You would know. Her mind presented a collage of society-page photos she'd seen of Taylor McQuaid with his debutante du jour at the Tulip Ball, the Snowflake Dance, the Sweetheart Soirée.

Yes, he'd know what flowers could do for a girl.

And he doesn't want to be ashamed of me if a photo of us is published somewhere, she thought. Besides, what could he ever see in her when he was the local escort for the cream of society?

The thought pierced her where she thought she was no longer vulnerable. She glanced down at the gardenia, and its heady scent engulfed her. "Thanks." Her voice had gone flat, and once again Taylor wondered what had happened to change her mood so abruptly.

The elevator doors opened, and several people filed out past them. Annie seized her opportunity and stepped inside. Her eyes met Taylor's briefly before the doors slid shut.

While Taylor used the room, Annie went to the hotel kitchen. She wrapped herself in a chef's apron, retrieved their casserole, and deposited it in an oven. Just before the casserole was thoroughly baked, she wrapped it with foil and slipped it into a warming oven until it was needed.

When it was time, a chef's assistant placed their casserole with others on a long buffet. With a sigh of relief Annie returned the apron and headed for the reception, which was already buzzing with people.

As she accepted a glass of champagne from a tray-bearing waiter, she saw Taylor enter the room. He looked handsome in his tuxedo and perfectly at ease, as if he wore one every day. From where she stood at the periphery, it was easy to watch heads turn in his direction. Clusters of celebrities and socialites alike opened to include him as he strode in. He nodded amiably to one and all and casually lifted a glass of champagne from a tray, his eyes scanning the room all the while.

Annie wished that she fit into this scene. For an instant she longed for the acceptance and warmth she saw extended to Taylor. She shook herself.

That was ridiculous. She wanted to be accepted all right, but in *art circles*—locally and in New York. She wanted to be appreciated for her talent and the ways she used it, not for her looks and social status. Yet she found herself admiring the way Taylor took it all in stride, nonchalantly, as if it were his due.

He's in his element, looking comfortable, confident, relaxed, she mused. And here I am on the sidelines, on the outside looking in.

His eyes found hers across the room, and above the heads of the people around him he nodded to her slowly. Her eyes softened as she returned the nod. With a smile and a murmur he extricated himself from a circle of acquaintances.

He wove through the throng with easy strides and joined her. Wordlessly he touched the rim of his glass to hers, and she heard a gentle clink. They looked into each other's eyes as they sipped from slender glasses.

"You look . . . ravishing," he said.

A small smile touched her lips. "I could say the same about you."

They turned as the master of ceremonies tapped the microphone. "Ladies and gentlemen, it's time for tasting." A room divider slid back dramatically, and the man gestured toward the endless buffet table, clothed in ivory damask and laden with dishes of all sorts. "Our celebrity panel will go through the line first, sampling everything. After they're finished tasting and voting, the rest of us can sample the dishes, if there's any left over."

There was a murmur of approval as a dozen celebrities formed a line, each with a huge, empty platter in hand. Slowly they worked down both sides of the table, selecting a few spoonfuls from every dish. Each celebrity was followed by an attendant who carried a scorecard and kept the portions arranged on the platter in the same order as the numbered items on the scorecard.

The celebrities took their platters to the head table, where they tasted and recorded their opinions on the scorecards. Eventually Annie and Taylor walked through the line. The variety of food was astounding. Annie wished the butterflies in her stomach were hungry, but they weren't. She sat across the table from Taylor, who seemed to have no trouble eating anything and everything.

"No sweat," he whispered, "ours is the best."

She shook her head. "You're not biased or anything."

He shrugged in a way that said time would tell.

Later, when the winning team was finally announced, Taylor looked at Annie with a look that said I told you so.

Though she'd heard their names clearly pronounced, she was amazed. "There must be some mistake." After she'd seen and tasted the foods they were up against, she'd given up all hope.

"I don't think so." Taylor nudged her elbow. "They're calling us."

As in a dream, Annie took a step, then two, until she was standing beside the master of ceremonies. She blinked at the sea of strangers, who were standing and applauding.

"And what do you call this masterpiece"—the man looked at the index card cupped inside his hand—"Miss Malone?"

She hesitated.

"Chicken Malone," Taylor said, smoothly filling in the gap.

"And Mr. McQuaid"—there was a measure of surprise in the speaker's voice—"just how much did you have to do with this delicious creation?"

"Very little, actually." There was laughter. "For

the most part I tried to stay out of the way." There was a ripple of applause.

Annie took a deep, steadying breath and glanced at Taylor out of the corner of her eye.

He's so good at this, so smooth, so self-assured, she thought. *I have to rise to the occasion. If he can, so can I.*

She straightened her shoulders and told herself to smile. Immediately she felt more confident, so that when the speaker handed her the Silver Spoon Award, a large silver ladle mounted on a block of wood, she took it, smiled brightly for the picture, and offered a gracious thank-you to everyone who had made the charity cookoff possible.

"And I'd like to dedicate our entry and this award to the memory of my mother, Annabelle Malone."

She felt a light but supportive squeeze from Taylor at her elbow, and again the crowd rose and applauded vigorously. They loved her. She could feel a wave of warmth rolling toward her. She was their darling, at least for this evening.

Annie and Taylor threaded their way through the tables, politely shaking hands and accepting kind, congratulatory words.

Abruptly Nathan Patrari rose from a table directly in front of them. "I can't believe you beat me," he muttered harshly.

Taylor looked him in the eye. "You beat yourself, Patrari."

The speaker tapped the microphone, and it made a loud popping sound. "May I have your attention please," he began. "There's something I forgot."

The crowd hushed, and Annie and Taylor turned toward the speaker.

"Miss Malone and Mr. McQuaid . . . the judges have just reminded me," he paused, looking a bit embarrassed, "to ask for your recipe."

The recipe. Annie stiffened in her tracks.

"If you'll please return to the microphone, I'm sure our guests are dying to hear your secret."

So am I, Annie thought as she glanced at Taylor.

At the microphone Annie cleared her throat. She could feel Taylor's presence beside her. At least he hadn't tried to desert her.

"Well," she began, "you start with boneless chicken breasts."

One of the judges, the editor of *Creative Cuisine*, stepped forward, leaned toward Annie, and whispered, "Just take out your recipe card, dear, and read it off." When a look of surprise crossed Annie's face, the woman continued, "Of course we'll publish it in our Christmas issue, but tonight's guests will want to copy your recipe down now. Makes them feel good to get the word first, you know."

Annie looked out to see people taking out notepads, clicking their ballpoints, then looking at her, their brows raised expectantly.

How could she tell them? They'd just applauded and congratulated her. Now she had to disappoint them, just when she was enjoying their approval. There was nothing to do but tell the truth. Annie's shoulders sagged, and she felt her heart sink like a lead weight. She swallowed against a dry throat and began cautiously, "Well, I don't actually have—"

"What Annie is trying to say," Taylor interrupted smoothly, "is that she didn't bring her recipe card with her." He raised his palms as if someone was holding a gun on him. "You can blame me. Since we'd already put the dish together this afternoon, I figured all we'd need to bring with us this evening was a little luck. Sorry," he added, looking like an errant schoolboy asking forgiveness. "We're new at all this."

People in the audience shrugged as they put away their notepads. Annie gazed up at Taylor in awe. This man could charm the birds from the trees, he was that suave.

The editor stepped to the microphone. "We'll forgive you this time, Mr. McQuaid. You can furnish us with your recipe tomorrow morning at our brunch."

The audience applauded.

Annie remembered that the finale to this weekend was a big brunch buffet provided by the hotel chef and his staff. Taylor McQuaid had just brought them a reprieve until the next morning.

After a half hour of polite conversation with well-wishers, Annie and Taylor made their way to the lobby. When they found themselves almost alone for a moment, he steered her to the elevators and quickly punched the button.

"Where are we going?" she asked.

He bent and said softly into her ear, "To the room."

Annie looked at him sharply. "Now, wait just a minute, if you think—"

"We have to talk," he interrupted in a harsh whisper, "alone."

Inside the elevator Annie jerked her elbow out of his grasp as the doors closed. "I thought I made myself clear on the subject."

"Perfectly." His voice was cool, and contained none of the debonair charm she'd heard flowing through the microphone, which only served to confirm her suspicion that he could turn the act off and on at will. "We have to get our game plan down."

"Of course. Enchant the people one minute and make fools of them the next." She wasn't sure if she was talking about the audience or herself.

He looked at her with a frown between his

brows. "I suppose you'd rather I'd left you at the microphone alone, groping for an explanation?"

When the elevator doors slid open, he stepped out and headed down the hall. She hesitated for a moment. The doors began to slide to a close. She shut her mouth and bolted out of the elevator. The doors closed shut behind her as she broke into a jog to catch up with him.

He'd left the door ajar, and it annoyed her as she stepped inside and closed it behind her that he was so sure she would follow him.

"Okay," she said, feeling more secure, "what's the deal?"

"The *deal* is that we have to get that recipe on paper." He walked to the bedside table and pulled open the drawer. Rummaging through it for a few seconds, he came up with a notepad and a stubby pencil. He sat on the bed, propped the pad on his knee, and looked at her expectantly.

She walked in the opposite direction and perched on a fireside chair.

"Okay," he said, scribbling busily, "first the chicken breasts. How many?"

"A pound . . . I think." At his steady look she threw her arms in the air. "I just look at the packages until I see one that looks big enough."

"A pound of boneless chicken breasts," he said firmly as he wrote it down.

"Better make that a pound and a half."

He sighed heavily as he made the correction. "Okay, sour cream." He glanced up. "How much?"

She leaned back and gazed at the ceiling. "Let's see, eight ounces in a carton . . . I use two cartons . . . no, sometimes more, sometimes less."

"Twenty-four ounces of sour cream," he said, writing it down.

"*Twenty-four ounces*! Wow, that sounds like a

lot. Just say two and . . . a half eight-ounce car-tons." She waved the air with one hand. "Sounds better that way."

He glared at her. "They don't furnish erasers on these pencils, you know."

She shrugged. "So scratch it out."

He bent his head and briskly rubbed the pencil across the paper. From across the room she could hear the lead snap.

"Damn!" He tossed the pencil onto the night-stand. "Why can't they give you a decent pencil in these places?" He pitched the notepad onto the bed as he bolted to his feet.

"This isn't going to work anyway," she said calmly.

He was pacing back and forth past the foot of the bed, his hands shoved into his pockets, his shoulders hunched. "You're telling me."

She ignored his rage, for some reason feeling calmer as he grew more upset. "The only way we're going to get the recipe down right is to make the dish again, weighing, measuring, and writing it down as we go."

He stopped and looked at his watch. "It's eleven thirty-five. Just how do you propose we do that?"

She stood up, sighing. "Follow me."

Seven

Minutes later they were knocking at an entrance to the hotel kitchen. Through a small window in the door they could see a cleanup crew loading dishes into the dishwasher across the room.

Taylor grabbed the handle and rattled the door. "This isn't getting us anywhere. It's locked, and they can't hear us over the noise in there."

"I've got another idea." Annie led the way into the banquet hall. Sure enough, busboys were still clearing the tables. Taylor followed her through a swinging door into the kitchen.

Annie paused to scan the large professional kitchen until she spotted the head chef pouring a thick liquid into an elaborate three-tiered copper mold. She strode to his side. "Oh, Chef Pierre, I'm so glad you're still here."

The stout, middle-aged man wearing a tall white toque stopped for a moment and looked at her until recognition dawned. "Congratulations, *chérie*, you won the cookoff!" He wiped his hand on his white apron before clasping her hand and

pumping it vigorously. "And you, too, *monsieur*."
He shook Taylor's hand. "Pretty soon you want my
job, *non*?"

Annie put her hand to her throat. "No way,
Pierre. Your job is safe from us."

"But you love to cook, *n'est-ce pas*? Some of
those people in my kitchen today"—Pierre shook
his head—"going through the motions only. But
with the two of *you*, I could see something special." He rubbed his fingers together. "A pinch of
this, and you taste, a splash of that, and another
taste. You put a little of yourselves into it, and so it
is you create a masterpiece." He lifted his shoulders and rolled his eyes. "I'm not surprised."

Annie touched his sleeve. "And that is exactly
why we need to ask you a favor."

Pierre's heavy brows lifted in surprise. "Ask."

"I want to give our recipe exactly as we per-
formed it today, here in your kitchen, but with all
our tasting and adding—well, we lost track of the
measurements." Her eyes darted to Taylor and
back to Pierre. "It wouldn't be fair to give approximate amounts."

Studying their faces, Pierre seemed to size them
up.

There was an awkward pause, and Annie spoke
to fill it. "If you're going to put your name on
something . . . and dedicate it to the memory of
someone . . . well, it ought to be the best you can
do."

Pierre nodded. "This I understand. But how may
I help?"

Taylor leaned forward. "Could we use your
kitchen to create the dish again?"

Pierre spread his arms. "But of course."

"Great," Taylor replied, turning to Annie. "I'll run
to the supermarket and be back in half an hour—"

"What's this?" Pierre interrupted. "You think I

do not run a well-stocked kitchen? You think my cupboard is bare?"

Taylor raised his hands. "I wouldn't presume . . ."

Chef Pierre lifted his chin, looking affronted and imperious at the same time. "I'll tell you what you may presume. Follow me." He led them into a storeroom stocked to the ceiling with enormous restaurant-sized containers of everything imaginable. He gestured grandly. "Tell my assistant Robert what you need, and he'll bring it to you. He'll be here mixing dough for the next few hours. I'll be going home soon."

Annie smiled into Pierre's eyes. "How can we ever repay you?"

Pierre cocked his head and regarded her with sparkling eyes. "Ah, I thought you'd never ask." He chuckled. "You could share your recipe, and perhaps leave a bit of your creation for my lunch."

Annie smiled. "You got it."

Pierre blew her a kiss as he turned to go.

Keeping a notebook handy, they began to assemble the ingredients and divide the tasks. They were bent over their work when from behind them they heard the clink of a bottle against a glass.

They turned to see Nathan Patrari lounging against a counter, a half-empty champagne bottle dangling in one hand and an overfull glass in the other.

Taylor released an audible breath in obvious displeasure. "What are *you* doing here?"

"I might ask you the same question, old buddy." Patrari raised up on his toes to peer at their preparations on the counter behind them. "I'd think you two could find something more interesting to do together than cook, cook, cook. Especially now"—he took a gulp of his champagne, weaving slightly—"that you've won." He lifted his glass in salute, and its contents sloshed over the sides.

"I'm surprised you're not out on the town." Taylor nodded at the door, hinting that now would be a good time for Patrari to go.

"All in good time." Their rival cocked his head. "I was just looking for you, McQuaid. Thought we'd share a li'l toast to your success. Of course, I can see that you're busy."

"Then you'll want to move right on," Taylor said crisply.

"I was just wondering"—Patrari took a sip— "how the rules of this little shindig go. Like if the winners don't produce a recipe, do the judges disqualify them and award the prize to their second choice?"

The atmosphere grew strained, and Annie turned around to lower the fire under the sizzling skillet.

Taylor glanced at Patrari. "I don't think the judges will have to bother with that."

Patrari shrugged. "Time will tell." He pushed himself away from the counter and chuckled as he sauntered away. "You two have fun now," he called out just before he disappeared through the swinging door.

A grim determination seized Annie and Taylor. For hours they tasted and added, amending the recipe every time, figuring amounts and refiguring.

Annie wiped her hands on her apron and looked up into Taylor's eyes to gauge the sincerity of his response. "Well, what do you think?"

"It's good."

She could tell he wasn't lying, but knew he was holding back. "But it's not quite right."

He leaned against the counter. "Well, it's as close to just right as we can get it."

Annie heaved a sigh and nodded. "If we fiddle with it much longer, we'll ruin it." A cream sauce could take just so much handling.

"If it makes you feel any better, we're the only ones who'll know that it's as close to being perfect, without being perfect, as it can get."

"What are we forgetting? What's different?"

He shrugged. "We're trying too hard."

She put a lid on the casserole, thanked the chef's assistant, and let him place it in the refrigerator. "We're keeping him here overtime."

Taylor nodded. "Time to pack it in."

She picked up the notepad. "I'll recopy this and hand it over tomorrow."

He walked out with her. While they waited for an elevator, he looked at her, and saw more than fatigue in her eyes. "It still bothers you."

"What?" she asked.

"That we didn't get it quite right."

She waited until they were alone inside the elevator. "I must seem like some weird, obsessive perfectionist."

"Nah." He paused to look as if he were rethinking it. "Well, a little weird perhaps."

She backhanded his shoulder playfully. "You're just trying to lighten me up, McQuaid."

"Me?" He faked a look of surprise as they stepped out of the elevator and started down the hall. "No way."

She looked up at him apologetically. "It was nice of you to stay up half the night helping out and being patient."

"Hey, quiet down. You'll ruin my reputation as a shallow, lecherous skirt chaser."

They exchanged a smile, then he watched her

expression grow solemn as they reached the door to the bridal suite.

There was a silent moment before he turned and put the key into the lock. This room was the only one to be had, and he hoped to dispel the sudden awkwardness between them in favor of the camaraderie they'd just shared. "Look, I know you're dying to have the fireside chairs all to yourself, but they're mine. You'll just have to make do with the bed."

"You had the chairs last night." He'd been fair with her; she'd be fair with him. "You take the bed."

"And let you have all the fun? Get outta here." He took her by the shoulders, turned her around, and gave her a gentle shove.

She looked at the bedside clock. "It's four o'clock in the morning." She turned to find him already sitting on one of the chairs, removing his shoes. With a weary sigh she realized that he'd made up his mind for them. "In a few hours we'll switch, and you can have the bed."

He leaned back and propped a pillow behind his head. "Are you going to talk all night, or are you going to turn off the light and let me get some sleep?"

"All right." She turned back the covers and switched off the bedside light. "Have it your way."

He shook his head in the dark. He was not having it his way. Not by a long shot.

Peeling one eye open and then the other against the glaring light, Annie rolled over and looked at the clock. It was ten A.M. She looked across the room to see Taylor slumped in one fireside chair, his feet resting on the other.

"Oh, no," she groaned. She'd fully intended to

trade places with him after a few hours, but she'd slept on through. She crawled out of bed and hurried to his side to shake him awake. "Taylor, it's your turn."

"What?" He looked at her groggily.

"Come on. It's your turn."

He closed his eyes and shook his head as if to clear it. When he opened his eyes, his gaze skimmed down her length. "My turn?"

It was then that she realized that all she was wearing was her pale silk camisole and bikini panties. It had been so late when they'd come in that she'd spared only enough time to slip out of her clothes and under the covers.

"Your turn in bed," she said hastily as she turned and hurried to the bathroom.

He watched her close the door and heard the click of the lock. "I knew it sounded too good to be true," he muttered, pushing himself up.

They hardly glanced at each other again until they were sitting side by side at the brunch an hour later. The editor of *Creative Cuisine* read the recipe for Chicken Malone into the microphone, while many scribbled it down.

Annie rose from the table to head for the buffet. Taylor was helping her with her chair when she saw Nathan Patrari stand up across the room. Following her glance, Taylor exchanged a look with Patrari. Then Nathan turned and walked from the room. A few seconds later Barlow rose and followed him.

Taylor touched Annie's elbow, and they walked to the long tables laden with assorted breads and rolls and bowls of fresh fruit. At the end of a row of warming dishes stood a chef preparing individual omelets to order.

A short distance away Chef Pierre stood watching everything, discreetly directing his morning staff. His eye caught Annie's as she placed her omelet order. Pierre sent her a small gesture, the fingers of one hand circling into an A-OK sign. At that moment she knew that he'd tasted the dish she and Taylor had prepared in the wee hours of the morning and left with a thank-you note for him. She smiled, and her shoulders sagged with relief. Her recipe had passed muster.

Annie and Taylor were quiet on the drive back, not jubilant from victory as she'd thought they would be. Annie was wishing they had hit upon the perfect combination as they had before, and though the concoction they'd made had been good enough to win, she felt at loose ends because it wasn't all she knew it could be.

Though she was reluctant to admit it, her melancholy mood had other origins. At the end of their return trip she might never see Taylor McQuaid again, and that eventuality bothered her.

There were no more cooking classes left to attend. And, of course, their weekend in Vail had not included the romance that he was surely accustomed to.

He'd already received the satisfaction of besting his archrivals, Patrari and Barlow. He probably wouldn't sign up for more cooking classes. For a man who traveled with the jet set, certainly the novelty of a gourmet cooking class would have worn off by now. So what incentive was there to see her again?

Taylor hadn't turned out to be the jerk that she'd thought he was at first. However, he was a handsome bachelor, and by his age obviously a *confirmed* bachelor. What could she expect if she got involved with a man like that? A whirlwind romance filled with empty promises, she answered her own question.

Annie glanced at him out of the corner of her eye. The wind through the open top of the car was ruffling his hair. She remembered running her fingers through his thick dark locks to remove the spiderwebs. She felt a sudden urge to reach up and rake her fingers through his hair now.

A lot of changes had occurred since they'd stopped to have their picnic on the way to Vail just a few days ago. But she had to admit that it was she who'd done the changing when she'd dropped her guard and let him grow on her.

She forced herself to look away. He was handsome—too handsome for his own good . . . or perhaps for her good. Men that good-looking attracted women whether they wanted to or not. Sooner or later they succumbed to temptation, no matter what they'd promised to whom. It was a fact she understood and accepted, and for that reason she was determined not to become a victim.

They drove through the breathtaking Rockies, pausing at Ute Pass to look down on a valley below where the meandering river looked like a silver chain under a turquoise sky.

Taylor gestured to the miles of lush pastures that stretched from the foothills of one mountain range to another. "The Ute Indians believed that God had promised this valley would be theirs forever. When this, too, was taken from them, they never got over it."

She shook her head sadly. "Promises don't last."

He studied her face curiously. "Sometimes they do."

When she shrugged, he could tell that she seriously doubted it. He shifted gears to first and eased out the clutch. "You're too young to be so pessimistic."

She lifted her chin a little. "Just realistic."

He headed down into the valley, glancing at a herd of horses just released for the winter. "All depends on your perspective." But he knew. He'd come to recognize, in the short time since he'd met her, when her defenses were being raised. And they were solidly in place. Like prison walls, he thought.

He left her to her thoughts and himself to his for the rest of the drive. At her apartment he lifted her bag out, and she insisted on carrying it upstairs herself. When they made their polite good-byes, he heard a finality in hers. Waiting in his car, he watched her climb the stairs, unlock her door, and close it behind her without a wave.

So, Ms. Annie Malone, you think you've seen the last of me, he said silently. *Use me to win your little cookoff and then a cool adiós? Well, babe, don't count on it.*

Adiós it was . . . for a brief two days.

He was driving around looking for a place to grab a late lunch on Friday. None of his old haunts looked appealing. Taylor didn't actually feel hungry, hadn't for the last two days. He just snacked off and on and ate a decent meal once a day, trying to get some of his old zip back. He'd lost his appetite, slept poorly, and snapped at his employees. Maybe he'd caught a bug.

Vitamins. All he needed was a megadose of C and some B complex. He turned down a few blocks, determined to double back to a little pharmacy where he could buy some vitamins.

It was then that he spotted the sign: COLLECTIBLE CARVINGS. There it was nestled in a corner of a cobblestone courtyard among several charming storefronts on a block the locals called Pickwick Plaza—Annie's shop.

Without thinking, he pulled to the curb and turned off the engine. He gazed at her shop window. The sign above it was hewn from the trunk of a mighty oak. And a few feet in front of it was a small trickling fountain. He was more familiar with the alley in back, but the shopfront was as pretty as he'd expected it would be.

Before he could give it a second thought, he was out of his car and walking through the wrought-iron entry. His footsteps clicked across the courtyard. Beside the door was a long park bench. He could almost imagine Annie sitting there whittling away.

Gazing at the window display, he saw two mallards, a pair of wood ducks, and a full-sized Canadian goose, each feather on every one of them so carefully carved and realistically painted that if he hadn't known better, he'd have sworn the whole flock was real.

Annie had carved them. He was sure of it, and his smile held more than a trace of pride. He decided it couldn't hurt to tell her how beautiful he thought they were. After all, the sign said visitors were always welcome.

He opened the door and stepped in. He didn't see anyone, but he figured that surely the tinkling bell over the door would summon her. "Hello," he called.

From a distance he could hear the roar of a motor. He browsed, his eye lighting upon one intricate carving after another. He couldn't believe the delicate detail of what looked like a woodland pool, a frog huddled on a lilypad in its midst. The longer he gazed at the scene, the more animals he discovered. The next table held an entire miniature western town.

He glanced up. The contrast in the back of the room startled him. A full-sized wooden Indian stood beside a table and chairs hewn from massive tree trunks, bark still clinging to the sides. The sound of a motor grew louder the deeper he walked into the long narrow store.

He ambled past the furniture all the way to the back and stopped in front of a wooden counter, bending over to view the tiny carvings inside the glass case below. As he straightened, he spotted an ornate antique brass cash register on the end. He leaned across the counter to get a look at all the keys on the other side. It was in perfect condition, one hundred years old if it was a day, a real dandy.

Suddenly the door beyond the counter flew open, and the muffled sound of a distant motor became a deafening roar. Taylor's eyes widened.

Filling the doorway was a mountain of a man in faded overalls, his dark eyes grim behind clear goggles, his long dark hair wild and disheveled, wood shavings and sawdust caught in his full beard. Dangling from one meaty fist was a chainsaw revving in thundering bursts.

The man's eyes moved accusingly from Taylor to the cash register and back again.

Taylor straightened, touching his chest with one finger. "You think that I . . . ?" He shook his head vigorously and raised his hands. "Just admiring, that's all, big guy."

Good grief, Annie'd never mentioned King Kong downstairs. Maybe that was why she was playing it cool. She already had Bigfoot for a boyfriend.

"Hey, the sign says visitors welcome," Taylor shouted over the din, watching the man slowly reach with his free hand for the handle of the chainsaw. "I called out when I came in," he continued loudly. The chainsaw suddenly stopped, and Taylor's words were ringing loudly in the aftershock of silence. "Nobody came," Taylor finished lamely. *Until now*, he thought, remembering scenes from a movie called *Chainsaw Massacre*.

The man slowly pushed his goggles to his forehead and set the hushed chainsaw on the counter. Then he removed a set of ear plugs. "What's that?"

Taylor released a long breath. "I'm a friend of Annie's."

The big man raised his heavy brows. "Yeah?"

"A friend from cooking class," Taylor said, not wanting to give him any wrong ideas.

The man's face creased into a hint of a smile as he looked Taylor up and down. "Yeah, she mentioned you."

Taylor swallowed, wondering what interesting details she might have included, such as their sharing the honeymoon suite at the Raphael. He glanced at the rugged teeth on the chainsaw and back to the giant. Somehow he didn't think Godzilla here would believe him about their separate sleeping arrangements. "I think I'll be going now. You might tell her McQuaid said hello. Nice place she has here."

Taylor heard a noise behind him and turned on his heel. "Hi," Annie said, "care for a sandwich?" She was carrying a plate holding several.

"No, thanks," Taylor replied.

Annie pushed the plate across the counter. "Sorry, I didn't hear you come in. I was upstairs fixing lunch. Sure you're not hungry?"

Taylor shook his head. There was an awkward pause.

"So," Annie began, "I guess you guys introduced yourselves."

"Not yet," the big man said, reaching across the counter. "I'm Bear Malone."

"Taylor McQuaid." Taylor shook his hand, trying

to keep from looking as shocked as he felt. She'd never told him she was married.

"I'm going back up for the iced tea." Annie looked at Taylor. "Would you prefer something else?"

"No, no, I'm not staying. Just dropped in to say hi."

"Stay here. I'll be right back." With that she bounded up the stairs and out of sight.

"Don't rush off on my account," Bear said. "You can stick around. I've got work to do."

Taylor eyed the chainsaw. *I'll just bet you do, and I'd rather it wasn't on me.*

"Besides," Bear continued, "she thinks I chase off all her boyfriends on purpose. Thinks I'm too protective and all."

"Oh," said Taylor, taking a step toward the door that seemed a million miles away.

"So, I might as well admit it," Bear said with a shrug, "I am protective where Annie's concerned."

Taylor took another casual step back. "You have every right to feel the way you do."

"Yeah." Bear's tone turned resolute. "Well, I might as well get this over with."

Taylor took a wide stance and stood his ground. If he had to die here and now, it wouldn't be without a helluva fight. He held up a hand in warning. "I think you'd better hold it right there."

"I like to settle things up front," Bear said, looking assessingly into Taylor's eyes. "That's my style. You see, I know your reputation. So, tell me, what are your intentions toward my sister?"

"Your *sister*?"

"Would you knock it off!" Annie marched down the stairs, carrying a large tray.

Taylor watched the big man's shoulders flinch as Annie nailed him with a glare. "Really, Bear, that's embarrassing."

"Sorry, Sis." Bear looked out the window and back at Taylor. "I apologize. I come on too strong sometimes."

"No apology necessary," Taylor said. "I'm sure I'd feel the same way if she were my . . . sister."

"I gotta wash up." Bear lifted the chainsaw from the counter as easily as if it were a toy. He turned and walked back through the doorway and closed the door behind him.

Annie looked at Taylor for a moment before setting the tray on the counter. "My brother is really a gentle person. He only said that because when I told him about our winning the cookoff, I made the mistake of mentioning that you know Nathan Patrari. As it turns out Bear has no use for Nathan."

Taylor smiled a little. "As it turns out, neither do I."

Annie chuckled. "Tea?"

"Thanks." Taylor accepted a glass and stood looking into her sea-green eyes, feeling as if it had been ten years since the last time he'd seen her.

"Your carvings are beautiful," he said, glancing around.

"Thank you."

"Your work is so delicate, so detailed." His gaze stopped when it came to the heavy furniture. "Well, most of it."

"Bear creates these out back, carves them free-hand with a chainsaw out of raw tree trunks." She took a seat on one of the tree chairs and offered one to Taylor.

"I think I heard him 'creating' when I came in." Taylor sat on a chair opposite hers, and leaned forward to whisper, "I'm afraid he suspects I came here to rob the cash register."

She whispered back, "I'm sure he doesn't think that now that he knows who you are."

"He doesn't trust me."

"He doesn't know you."

Taylor looked into her eyes, his own full of questions. Did *she* trust him? Did *she* know him?

She broke eye contact first, glancing down at the iced-tea glass in her hand, twisting it, blotting it on the knee of her jeans. "Bear and I don't have much family except each other. We're a little slow to warm up to strangers, I guess."

"Surely you don't still think of me as a stranger?" He took a long swallow of tea.

"No. And perhaps, like my brother, I'm too prone to make snap judgments."

"You're forgiven."

She couldn't help but smile. "I wasn't apologizing."

"I know."

She shook her head. He was still full of surprises . . . and charm.

"Well"—he handed her the half-empty glass—"I won't wear out my welcome."

She followed him to the door. He paused by her workbench near the front. Her current project was there, still in the beginning stages, but he recognized the photo propped up beside her tools. He gently picked it up and held it to the light.

It was a picture taken of a golf course, a doe and her fawn pausing in front of the seventh green, a triangular flag whipping in the background. The memory flooded back for both of them—his warm hands clutching her waist as she'd balanced precariously out of the top of his car, camera poised, shutter snapping; that fleeting glimpse they'd witnessed and shared; the flush of enthusiasm on her face when she slid down onto the seat beside him. Nostalgia tugged at him now, just looking at the photograph.

He handed the picture to her and smiled. "Special," he said.

The corners of her mouth curved, and her eyes softened. He knew what that moment had meant to her.

He waved as he walked out the door.

She looked down at the photo in her hand. It held a scene others would have passed without so much as a second glance, but he appreciated that for her those sights were small miracles.

Without being told, he had somehow understood.

Eight

Annie carefully loaded the large box of carved miniatures in her car and closed the hatchback. The owner of Nina's Interior Design had asked her to bring over an assortment to arrange in the firm's showrooms and display homes.

This wasn't the big break she longed for, but it was a start, another outlet for her work. Her carvings would be seen by more people. As it was, only those who came into her shop knew of her talent. She smoothed the back of her dress as she slid into the driver's seat. It was important to look nice, and to be on time. Her appointment at Nina's was at nine A.M. Annie glanced at her watch and felt proud of herself. She was leaving a half hour early.

"See, you can do it," she told herself. "From now on you're going to start out this early for every appointment, drive within the speed limit, and arrive with time to spare. Never again will your heart be racing through traffic, never again will you arrive looking like you just finished the Boston Marathon."

She was going to change her ways. It wasn't that she hadn't valued punctuality or that she hadn't known it was impolite to be late. She'd just always had a habit of thinking she had more time than she actually did. Absorbed in whatever she was doing, she'd suddenly realize that she had two minutes to be somewhere. It was an embarrassing habit, and unprofessional too.

She turned the key and waited a moment while the engine warmed up, then backed up and drove down the alley and out onto the street. Shifting into second gear, she applied a little more gas. Her little compact was nothing special, but it usually had a bit more pep than this.

She shifted into third, eased out the clutch, and pressed the gas pedal. Still no speed. How long had it been since the last tune-up? She shrugged as she shifted into fourth. Car maintenance wasn't her thing.

It wasn't her brother's thing either. He didn't even own a car. Something about his not contributing to the breakdown of the ozone layer. Bear Malone walked, hitched rides, and when he got desperate, took the bus. The only motor he maintained was in his chainsaw.

Annie smiled when she thought of that. For some reason, Bear was convinced that his chainsaw did not contribute to air pollution—noise pollution, perhaps, but not air pollution.

At the third stoplight Annie's car took off slowly, a rare sight in Colorado Springs. It was increasingly more sluggish after the next light. She was beginning to worry.

"Come on, Streak, don't do this to me now. Get temperamental tomorrow or next week, but not now." She pressed the gas hard. The car lunged and lurched and nearly died on the spot. "Okay, okay," she said soothingly. "I'll be nice."

For the next five blocks Annie babied her car along—no sudden stops, no sudden starts. But seven blocks later, she knew she was in trouble. The Streak coughed and nearly died at three stoplights in a row. By now Annie was scanning the street for a garage. "Where's a service station when you need one?" she muttered.

She spotted the huge garage doors of a service area attached to a new-car dealership. Needing help fast, she whipped onto the lot.

Heads turned as her car lurched and sputtered past rows of shiny new cars. Despite her embarrassment, it dawned on her that these shiny new cars were an assortment of the finest luxury sports cars in the world. She glanced up at the sign high in the air. McQuaid's it said in bold red script.

"Great," Annie muttered, "just great." She hadn't seen Taylor McQuaid since he'd dropped into her shop two weeks ago. The last thing she wanted was for him to get the idea that she was pursuing him.

She pulled into line at the service area and rolled down her window as a white-coated attendant approached. He leaned down to look in at her.

"May I help you, ma'am?"

Annie turned the key to shut off the ignition, but the motor continued to rattle and knock for a full minute. She closed her eyes tightly until the racket stopped, feeling mortified. *Why me? Why now? Why here?*

She looked at the attendant. "Can you fix it?"

"Sure thing." The young man opened her door for her.

"I have an appointment in fifteen minutes." There was a hint of panic in her voice.

"No problem. Our courtesy van is back from the eight-o'clock run. We can fill out the paperwork and have you on your way in five minutes."

"Wonderful." Annie glanced at the tinted windows of the showroom, hoping that Taylor McQuaid wasn't standing inside watching. She shook her head. Don't be silly, she told herself, the boss probably doesn't drag in till noon.

"Is there anything you need to take with you?" The young attendant was looking at the assorted clutter in the backseat and floor.

Annie swallowed against a dry throat. She'd meant to clean out her car for a month now, but there was never enough time to tackle the chores she hated.

"I have a box in the back." She started to lift the hatchback, but the young man took over.

"I'll do that for you, ma'am," he said smoothly. "This box?"

"If you could keep it level—"

"No problem."

She slipped the strap on her handbag over her shoulder and followed him to the service desk. As he'd promised, they had the paperwork filled out in short order. He pointed to a gray van parked in front of the showroom. "I'll tell the service manager you need a ride, and he'll send a driver out right away." He lifted the box from the counter between them. "Here, I'll carry this out for you."

Annie reached for the box. "No need. It's not heavy, and you have other customers to see." He sent her an appreciative nod and beckoned to the man waiting in line behind her.

Annie took her box and strode outside quietly. Two men in navy coveralls were pushing her car into a work bay. She glanced away, looking as though she'd never seen that car in her life. The Streak had brought her enough attention for one day. Though no one here had snickered or been unkind to her, she felt humiliated. Her car sure looked like a clunker in a ritzy dealership like this.

She hurried out to the van. To her relief, it was empty. She climbed into the front passenger seat and set her box on the first bench seat behind her. Checking her watch, she calculated that if the van pulled out now, she'd barely make it to Nina's Interior Design on time.

She dreaded having to explain her lateness with the same old lame excuse of car trouble. Most people didn't even believe that one anymore.

Glancing at her watch again, she felt doubts closing in. Perhaps the nice young attendant had forgotten to tell the service manager to get the driver. Maybe she should go back inside and double-check. That was the last thing she wanted to do, but her frayed nerves wouldn't permit her to wait much longer.

She opened the door and had one foot on the step bumper when she heard the door to the driver's side opening and caught a glimpse of a man swinging into the seat beside her.

"Thank goodness you're here," she murmured, closing her door. When she turned to give the driver the address, her eyes widened.

"Good to know you missed me," Taylor said smoothly, turning the key in the ignition. "Where to?"

"Nina's Interior Design."

"I know the place." He reversed the van and pulled to the street to wait for a break in traffic.

She stared at him, unable to believe her eyes.

"It's not polite to stare," he reminded her playfully without taking his eyes off the traffic.

She blushed, remembering how she had chided him with the same words on the way to cookoff. "Excuse me. I just didn't expect the boss to be driving the courtesy van."

He chuckled. "What do you think I do? Sleep till noon and then go for a manicure?"

"Something like that."

"Well, actually when I'm not around, I'm the only one who doesn't need a substitute. If you think about it, that basically makes me the least important person there. So when someone is out with the flu or whatever, I fill in where needed, at least through our busy times."

She shook her head. "I can't see you in greasy coveralls rushing around changing oil in twenty-five minutes or less."

"Stick around. I'm pretty fast."

She batted her eyes at him. "Tell me about it."

They both chuckled and then fell silent, thinking about that long-ago morning when she was in his arms on the honeymoon bed.

A small light flashed on a two-way radio mounted below the dash. "Taylor? Come in, Taylor."

He lifted the mouthpiece and pressed a button. "Roger. This is Taylor. Come in, Sally."

"We've gotten an emergency call from the Children's Home. The school bus has broken down again, and the kids need a ride pronto or they'll be late for school. Can you do it?"

Taylor's eyes went to Annie, and he released the button so that they wouldn't be heard. "How about it? Can you spare a few minutes? It's on our way."

Glancing at her watch, she opened her mouth to tell him that she'd barely make her appointment as it was, then she sighed and shrugged. "Okay." It seemed whether she started out early or not, she was doomed to be a late arriver.

A few minutes later Taylor pulled up in front of a long concrete-block building. The front door flew open, and ten children filed out, heading for the van. Taylor hopped out and slid open the side door. As the kids piled in on the three bench seats,

Annie scooped up her box of miniatures and set it on the floor behind the center console.

"Hey, Taylor, when we goin' fishin' again, huh?" shouted the tallest youngster, a boy who looked to be of American Indian descent.

"The circus," called another, "let's go back to the circus."

A thin boy in the last seat stood to be heard. "Swimmin'," he said, "we could go swimmin' like before."

"No," shouted the tallest, "too cold for swimmin' now, you dummy, unless you wanna freeze your—"

"Remember the rules, guys," Taylor interrupted as he swung into his seat. "Buckle up and watch your language around the lady."

"Oh, sorry," said the tall boy, noticing Annie for the first time. "Who are you?"

"This is Annie Malone," said Taylor, turning the ignition key. "You gentlemen introduce yourselves."

As they began, a stout, middle-aged woman walked out of the building and up to Taylor's window. "Thanks again," she said. He nodded, and she pointed to the yellow bus in the driveway. "It isn't the new battery you put in. I'm afraid it's something major this time." Her face looked grim.

"I'll tow it in this afternoon, Mrs. Henderson, when things slow down in the shop. We'll see what we can do."

The woman shook her head. "Thanks. We'd been afoot a long time ago if you hadn't coddled it along for years. I don't know what we'll do if it's really shot this time."

"Well, maybe the Jaycees can buy you another this year if our telethon pans out."

"Sure hope so, Taylor." She waved as he backed out of the drive.

"Hey, what's in there?" The tall boy, whose name

was Chip, pointed to the box Annie had set on the floor. "Doughnuts?"

Taylor glanced down. "That belongs to the lady."

"Can we see?" Chip nudged the corner up with the toe of his sneaker.

By Taylor's change of expression, Annie could sense a scolding coming on—he'd seen Chip's move. "Sure," she said smoothly, lifting the lid. "Sorry, they're not edible."

The boys peered over the seat to get a look. "Gosh, those are cool," said the towheaded Jeff. "Where'd you get 'em?"

"I carved them out of wood."

The boys looked closer. "With a knife?" asked Chip, his eyes lighting with interest.

She nodded. "With tools made for the job."

"They look like little people," said a voice in the back. "Could you hold 'em up so we can see?"

As Annie held up the figures one at a time for the youngsters' inspection and critiques, Taylor pulled up in front of the school. He climbed out to slide open the door, then the older boys descended in pairs from the van. " 'Bye, Annie," they called. "See ya, Taylor. Thanks."

Then it was time for the three little ones in the jump seat in the back to unload. Taylor lifted them down, one after another. The last one turned and scrambled back into the van behind Annie. "Can I see?" he asked softly. "They wouldn't let me see."

Annie lifted the lid. The child's eyes widened. He reached out tentatively with one finger. "Can I touch?"

She nodded and placed the carving of a little boy in the palm of his hand.

"Oh," he said in awe. His eyes grew sad as he held it out to her. "It's beautiful."

The child looked young, yet his pale blue eyes

looked old and haunted. Annie folded his fingers over the carving still in his hand. "It's yours."

The child's eyes lit with hope, then darkened with doubt. "For me?"

She nodded.

"I wanna make something like this. Maybe I'll get me a knife out of the kitchen and some old sticks."

She shook her head. "Don't do that. It's too easy to cut yourself if you don't learn how to carve properly."

His face fell.

"Tell you what, if you come to my shop, I'll teach you how to carve the right way."

His face brightened. "Me? Just me? Could Taylor bring me?"

Annie twisted in her seat to look at Taylor, and he nodded. She looked at the little boy. "If it's all right with the people where you live."

"Sure. Miz Hendersen don't care."

Taylor put his hand on the boy's shoulder. "You'll have to do your homework first."

The boy nodded. "I will." Then he looked at Annie. "Thanks."

She smiled at him. "What's your name?"

"Everybody 'round here calls me Squirt . . . but my real name is Brian."

"Well, Brian, you can call me Annie."

He looked up at her shyly. "Can I come over on Saturday?"

She smiled at him and nodded. "If it's okay with Taylor and Mrs. Henderson."

Brian turned pleading eyes to Taylor.

"Okay, Saturday it is," he said, "but you'd better scoot. You're late for class."

Brian glanced again at Annie. "'Bye," he said softly as he hopped out of the van.

She watched him lug his book bag up the sidewalk, the carving still tucked tightly into his little fist.

When Taylor turned on the ignition, she swung her gaze to him. "How old is Brian?"

"He's nine."

"He's so small for his age!"

Taylor nodded. "He's had a rough start on life. He's been at the Children's Home for about six months"—he swiveled to look at her directly—"and I can tell you that that's the most anyone's heard him say since he arrived."

"You must spend quite a bit of time with the boys."

"I enjoy it."

She looked straight ahead thoughtfully as he pulled into traffic. "He sounds like he wants to come over without the others."

"So far, he's been a loner. I try to take the boys for activities in groups of two or three, and individually when I can. Those boys have to do so much sharing of everything, it's no wonder when one of them longs to be singled out for something special." He glanced at her, and the look in his eyes was warm. "I think you're something special for Brian."

She shook her head, a hint of a smile on her lips. "You never cease to amaze me, McQuaid."

Annie was relieved that Nina was too delighted with her carved miniatures to make a fuss about her late arrival. When she ordered another two dozen, Annie was pleased.

"Wasn't that Taylor McQuaid who carried your package in here?" Nina asked casually as she wrote up the order.

Annie nodded. "I had car trouble this morning, and he was driving the courtesy van."

"He *was*. Well, imagine that, Taylor McQuaid driving the courtesy van when he can take a Jag or Porsche or anything he wants."

Annie crossed the room, pretending to be interested in a figurine, hoping that Nina would drop the subject.

"Taylor McQuaid," Nina said dreamily. "What every single woman wouldn't give to snag him. Quite a catch."

"I wouldn't know." Annie set down the figurine too quickly, and the sound echoed. "Sorry." She suddenly felt unsettled, and was not sure why.

"Is he going to pick you up too?"

"What?" asked Annie, giving the figurine a quick inspection to be sure she hadn't hurt it any.

"I asked if Taylor McQuaid was picking you up here. You did say your car was in the shop, didn't you?"

"Uh, yes, it is." Taylor had offered to come get her; all she had to do was call. But at this moment, that was the last thing she wanted to do. She didn't need the grapevine buzzing about her, linking her name with Taylor's, speculating on how long his dalliance with an artist could last.

She'd tried to stay out of the mainstream, out of the gossip channels, devoting her time instead to her work while she studied with some of the best local artists. Never wanting to be the talk of the town, she'd always preferred to be respected for who she was and not for whom she was dating.

Glancing out the front window, she spotted a bus stop at the corner. "I'm taking the bus back," she told Nina. "Do you happen to know the schedule?"

The bus ride home gave Annie time to think. Taylor was much more than she'd expected of him. In so many ways he was nothing like the local perception of him. He was kind, thoughtful, generous, and rather unpretentious. But that playboy reputation clung to him, perhaps because of his friends, perhaps because of his cars, and—though she hated to admit it—perhaps because of his women.

The better she got to know him, the more she felt drawn to him. But to become involved with Taylor McQuaid would be a mistake on her part. Friendship should be her object. If they could remain platonic friends, then maybe the relationship would last for more than a few weeks or months. Logic and experience told her that being Taylor's girlfriend might be thrilling, but wouldn't last.

She had plans and dreams. The last thing she needed in her life was upheaval and heartbreak. She was not the type who could play around. When she fell in love, it would be wholeheartedly.

That afternoon she called the dealership and found out that her car was ready. She walked several blocks to the bus stop. Bear had filled her in on the routes, and after switching buses twice, she arrived at McQuaid's.

The same young man who'd helped her that morning approached her at the service desk. "Your repairs are finished, but it will be a few minutes. At the moment our crew is washing and vacuuming your car."

"I didn't order a wash."

"Comes with the service, ma'am."

Annie was scanning the bill for the charge, but no charge for a wash had been tacked on. They didn't throw in any freebies at the place where she usually took her car. And to her surprise, even the repair charges were reasonable.

"So it's running again," she said as she wrote out a check.

"Yes, ma'am, the boss tested it personally this afternoon."

"Isn't that a little unusual?" The words were out of her mouth before she could stop them.

"Not really, ma'am. He takes a personal interest in every department. If you'd like, there are complimentary refreshments in our lounge."

Annie gazed past him through the open bay doors. It was a glorious autumn afternoon. "I think I'd rather wait outside."

The young man smiled, and she walked through the doorway to the back, pausing for a moment to gaze at Pike's Peak. It took her gaze into the clouds and beyond. In places, the white puffy clouds blocked the sun, causing huge splotches of shade on the mountain.

Behind the car agency was a wooded area where the grass between the huge firs and spruce had been mowed like a park. She wandered outside, then caught sight of a yellow school bus parked in the shade of the building. Curiosity drew her to the side of the bus. Bold black letters told her what she'd suspected: CHILDREN'S HOME, COLORADO SPRINGS.

A groan came from beneath the bus, as a man in grease-stained coveralls rolled out from under it. As he climbed to his feet, she recognized Taylor McQuaid.

"Damn," he muttered.

"That bad, huh?" she asked, sensing the cause of his frustration.

Startled, he spun around. A smile split his face when he saw her, then his face sobered as he glanced at the bus. "Afraid so. Her motor is on its last legs, and we've patched her body to the point of no return. It's time to scrap her and buy another."

"Can they afford it?"

"No." He pulled a rag from his hip pocket and started wiping the grease from his hands. "That's why we've been babying it along."

Her head tilted as she looked up at him, seeing him in a different way, admitting to herself finally that there was a great deal more to this man than his playboy image.

"What are they going to do?" she asked. "They've got most of the school year to go, haven't they?"

He nodded, looking a bit tired. "The school district will pick up the kids for now, but the home needs a vehicle to haul them other places too. We're planning a charity benefit to raise the funds for a good used bus—a safe, reliable one." He patted the old yellow-coated metal with the flat of his hand. "I have some ideas."

"I'll bet you do."

His head turned in her direction, not because she'd sounded sarcastic, but because she had not. Her voice had always before held a hint that she saw him as a shallow hotshot perpetually angling for his next female conquest, herself included. He'd always recognized that knowing, I've-got-you-pegged tone and it annoyed the hell out of him. But now her tone of voice was utterly benign, and the way she was looking up at him resembled something close to admiration.

Even covered with grease and dirt, Taylor still looked handsome to Annie. His eyes were bluer than the Colorado sky as he wiped his brow and started toward his pocket with the rag. On impulse she reached to take it from him. She rubbed a smudge from the straight bridge of his nose and then dabbed a spot in the cleft of his chin.

"There," she said with a gentle smile that faded as her gaze met his. The indulgent look in his eyes held an intimacy that caught her off guard. She forgot to breathe as he stepped closer. Suddenly the crisp air turned sultry. Her heart began thumping so hard, she could feel it pulsing in her ears, shutting out the twitter of birds overhead and the clanging that echoed inside the service area nearby.

His face was only inches from hers when he paused, his gaze moving from her wide eyes down to her lips, which trembled slightly. They both knew that this was her chance to object, to step back . . . and they both knew when that instant had passed.

Without touching her anywhere else, he brought his lips to hers. His kiss was soft, tentative, undemanding. She found herself swaying toward him, wanting just a little more. All the while a dim voice somewhere in the back of her head urged her to quit now, move away, pretend nothing had happened, but the message sounded faraway and muddled, a message she didn't want to hear, not now.

His lips moved over hers again, this time with more feeling. He kissed her over and over again, exploring, tasting, savoring. Her hands came to rest on his shoulders, perhaps for balance, perhaps to be sure that this heady madness didn't stop too soon.

She might not let herself get involved with him, but she wouldn't go through life wondering what it was like to kiss and be kissed by him. The last time he'd kissed her, she'd ended it prematurely, trying to block the feelings only he could draw from her. But this time she was fully aware of every sensation, the welling of deep need rising upward within her, the hunger that seemed to increase even as it was fed.

She returned his kiss with a fervor that surprised them both. He hadn't meant to touch her, but his arms came around her, drawing her tightly against him. The weeks of waiting came to an end—the hours of brushing against her as they worked side by side without ever reaching out to squeeze her, the moments of victory passing by without a hug—all these were swept away in an embrace made all the dearer for having been denied so long.

So many times he'd started to reach for her, not to be amorous, but to be affectionate. But the look in her eye, the tone in her voice, had kept him at arm's length. Her defensive attitude had always quashed his natural impulse to be playful and spontaneous.

But at this moment there was more than affection, more than attraction, there was tenderness . . . and passion. He couldn't get close enough to her, couldn't kiss her long enough. He wanted to be somewhere far away, alone with her for hours.

She felt it, too, as her hands plunged into his thick hair, pulling his head down to hers. Kissing his mouth with an abandon she'd never known, she marveled. Where had it come from, this wellspring of passion? She'd only meant to sample, to taste, perhaps to memorize, his lips, for the days—the years—of aloneness ahead. But one kiss had required another, until all she wanted was to be alone with him to explore, to discover more.

It was beginning to dawn on her that it was impossible to experiment with Taylor McQuaid without becoming obsessed.

"Miss Malone?" The voice came to her from a distance, and it took a few seconds for her to recognize it. "Miss Malone, we have your car—"

The voice of the young white-coated attendant stopped in midsentence when he spotted her in the arms of Taylor McQuaid. The young man discreetly disappeared back inside, just before Annie guiltily jumped away.

She raked her fingers through her hair and bent

forward to inhale a deep breath. Taylor's hands reached for her shoulders, to steady, to comfort.

She brushed them away. "No, I have to go," she said breathily but with conviction. "I have to . . . get my head on straight."

"It's okay," he said, sensing her confusion, wanting to reassure her somehow that it was okay to let herself open up, let herself live.

She waved him away. "I have to go now." A tinge of desperation entered her voice. She had to get away now to get her equilibrium back, to get some sense of balance. Turning, she started away without another word.

"See you Saturday," he said.

Her steps faltered for an instant. She was going to tell him to forget about that too.

"See you Saturday," he repeated, "or there will be one disappointed little boy." And one disappointed grown man, too, but he didn't tell her that.

She took two steps while she wrestled with the guilt of hurting a little boy who'd probably felt rejected far too many times already. She kept walking, not looking back, putting more distance between them, as she nodded. "Okay, Saturday, then."

Nine

For three days Annie debated about calling Taylor and canceling Saturday. But every time she picked up the phone to make her excuse, she saw Brian's sad, wary eyes looking at her. If she canceled, she would only add to his feelings of disillusionment and rejection. Still, when she remembered how she felt in Taylor's arms that one crazy afternoon, she grew desperate to put time and distance between them.

What had happened to her resolve not to get involved with him? Gone like the morning mist, she thought, feeling disgusted by her own weakness. True, Taylor McQuaid wasn't the cad she'd thought he was. She'd learned, however reluctantly, that he was an unassuming, generous, kindhearted man. But that didn't change the fact that he traveled in different circles, that he had friends she found off-putting, that he had more charm and good looks than one man was entitled to have. He attracted women without effort, and gossip followed him whether he liked it or not. He never stayed with any one woman—why should he, when there were always so many others, waiting in the wings?

She couldn't get involved with him. She was a failure in the casual-affair department. If she understood anything about herself, it was that. Many artists could live a Bohemian lifestyle, taking on and discarding lovers without a second thought; she simply could not. Sometimes she wished she could; it would make life simpler. She couldn't even take in a stray cat without falling in love with it. How in the world could she hang out with Taylor McQuaid without falling for him?

Until a few days ago when she'd kissed him, she'd believed that she could spend time with him while keeping their relationship on a purely platonic level. She'd been kidding herself. While she stalked around her shop, sweeping up, putting her tools into their holders, she raged at fate.

Why did it have to be him? Why couldn't the guy down the street make her feel that way? Why Taylor McQuaid? A surefire heartbreaker if there ever was one!

Her eyes went to the large school clock on the wall. It was ten o'clock in the morning. Maybe Taylor wouldn't show. That prospect flooded her with relief while it tormented her with disappointment. Caught in a mire of conflicting emotions, she stormed to the front door and lifted the shade to flip the sign from CLOSED to OPEN.

At that moment she looked up and saw him through the window in the door, standing on the doorstep, his blue eyes studying hers, young Brian's hand tucked into his. In the man's face she saw a somber mixture of hope and uncertainty; and in the boy's face, the same to a greater degree.

She opened the door and formed a smile. "Good

morning, gentlemen." She stepped back. "Come in."

The child's eyes filled with wonder as he walked into the shop, his head twisting back and forth, taking in everything, his hand still tightly gripping Taylor's. They followed Annie to her work corner.

She perched on a bench to make direct eye contact with Brian. "Would you like something to drink or a cookie?" she asked him.

He shook his head, then glanced up at Taylor and back to Annie. "Uh, no, thank you."

She glanced up at Taylor. "Would you?"

"No, thanks, we just finished dining at the Golden Arches."

Annie smiled in spite of herself.

"Is this where you made the little boy you gave me?" Brian inquired.

She nodded. "I do a lot of carving right here. The customers enjoy watching, and I can get a lot done when business is slow."

Brian slipped his hand from Taylor's and began to wander here and there, looking at everything. He locked his fingers together and glanced frequently at Taylor, who nodded to him approvingly.

"I take it you two have an agreement," she said softly, turning her head in Brian's direction. Looking at the child was safer than looking at the man.

"We had a talk about manners over breakfast," Taylor said quietly, watching the boy. "He's trying very hard not to touch without permission." *And so am I*, Taylor thought as he gazed at her, the corners of his mouth lifting in a wry smile.

Brian was drawn to the folk toys. A row of them were lined up on a driftwood log suspended between two tables. Impulsively, he reached out, and then remembered. His hand stopped in midair. "Is it okay," he began tentatively, "to rock it . . . a little?"

Brian was pointing at a six-inch carving of a little old man poised atop the log. It was a replica of an early American toy, a carving of a log splitter, complete with a tiny ax between his hands. Out of his back came a wire that curved out and went under the log, with a small block attached on the end, balancing the toy like a pendulum.

"Go ahead," Annie said with a smile, "that's what it's for."

Brian gave the little man a push with his finger, and the figure bobbed up and down, looking as if he were chopping the driftwood log beneath his feet, the balancing block below swinging to and fro.

Brian's eyes lit up, and his face split with a grin. Annie's heart swelled as she watched his look of sadness magically transformed to delight as he played with the toy that she'd carved herself.

He looked at her, his mind made up. "I want to make one like this."

"You're sure?" she asked.

"Oh, yeah." He gave the toy another push and giggled softly as the log splitter bobbed up and down, looking as if he was chopping wood for all he was worth.

"That looks kind of tricky," Taylor said in an undertone that only Annie could hear.

She nodded thoughtfully. "I think you can manage it."

Taylor did a double take. "What? Me?"

"I thought you'd want to join the class." There was a glint of challenge in her eye as she tilted her head to look up at him.

Brian walked toward them, his voice high with excitement. "Oh, boy! Taylor can learn with me." His heart held enough enthusiasm for both of them, and Taylor found himself shrugging in agreement. "Great!" Brian said.

Taylor found it impossible to refuse when the boy looked happier than he'd ever seen him, so he took his place as Annie directed, across the work table from her. Brian stood close to her side.

"Okay." She began by handing a block of wood to each of them. "Bear cuts these out for me with the band saw."

The rough blocks were about the shape and size of the toy, but other than that bore little resemblance to the finished product.

"Run your fingers over the wood, get to know it," she said. "Feel it to find the direction of the grain."

Instinctively, Brian ran his fingers up and down the block of wood.

"That's right," she said. "We cut it with the grain so that the block is stronger. We try not to use knots and weak places, but every piece of wood has its own personality."

"Just like people?" Brian asked.

She nodded. "Just like people. Each has its own character, and its strength and weakness in a different place. You never know what it will be like until you get into it and get to know it. Each has its quirks. No two are exactly alike."

"So," Taylor interjected, "I think what you're saying is we should explore each one carefully." He looked at her pointedly. "In the same way, it would be unwise for us to assume we know what someone is like without discovering his 'quirks' for ourselves. Is that what you mean, Annie?"

She swallowed, looking away. "Something like that."

"Go on," he said. "I'm fascinated."

She glanced down to avoid his penetrating gaze and pointed to the raised wooden frames nailed to the table in front of each of them. "It's important to brace your work against the bench hook when you're working on it. That will keep the block steady so that you can use both hands on the carving tool. If you keep one hand on the wood and one hand on the tool, you're more likely to cut yourself."

Brian watched Annie and braced his block against the right angle of the corner the way she did. She handed each of them a pencil and took one for herself.

"Now," she said, "we'll draw on the woodcutter's arms right about here." She drew two parallel lines onto her block, and Brian and Taylor did the same on theirs.

"Like this?" Brian asked.

"That's good," she said. "You don't have to worry about being exact when you're carving folk art."

She handed out U-shaped tools. "This is a macaroni tool," she said. "We'll use it to remove the wood around the arms so that they stand out."

Brian watched her demonstrate and imitated her moves. He pursed his lips as he concentrated on each stroke. She glanced up to see a similar expression on Taylor's face as he worked.

"Just like that," she said. "Always keep your fingers behind the tool and you won't cut yourself."

Brian and Taylor worked away, shaping and rounding, the wood peeling in curls in front of their chisels.

"This is fun," said Brian, glancing up at Taylor.

"Yeah," Taylor said wryly as he dug too steeply and the chisel hung up.

Annie circled the table to stand beside him. Her hand closed over his, guiding his hand back. "Easy does it," she said soothingly. "Just let it glide across the wood. Don't force it."

Her face was close to his, and he couldn't resist looking at her. When she glanced at him, her throat closed convulsively. It seemed she couldn't get near him anymore without reacting to that magnetic pull. Her hand trembled on his slightly.

"I think I can handle it," he said, sounding more defensive than he'd intended, and Annie returned to her place beside Brian.

"Don't feel bad," Brian whispered earnestly to Taylor. "Lots of kids don't catch on real fast at school."

Annie's mouth twitched as she suppressed a smile. Brian had intended to comfort Taylor, but his comment had packed a punch.

"Calling your old buddy a slow learner?" Taylor asked, his macaroni tool hanging up again.

Brian's brow wrinkled as he looked at Taylor. "You always tell us that learning slow is better than not learning at all."

"That sounds like something I'd say, all right." Taylor glanced at Annie, looking a bit chagrined. "It's great when your words come back to haunt you."

"Tell me about it," she said, thinking that she'd done nothing but break her own rules since the day she'd met him.

Annie and Brian watched Taylor back up the gadget and smooth his strokes the way she'd shown him. She passed out another tool with a small grooved channel, and they followed her lead, hewing out the shape of the little man's hat and his bushy eyebrows.

"Mine's face doesn't look like yours," said Brian, holding his carving next to Annie's.

"It doesn't have to," she reassured him.

Taylor held up his. "Mine doesn't look like any-body's."

Annie nodded. "I'd have to agree with you there."

Taylor's jaw dropped in an expression of mock dismay, and Brian giggled at their goodnatured banter. Annie handed out short-bladed knives. "Now it's time to sit down and do a little whittling."

They followed suit and sat down on benches. "We hold the wood in one hand and the knife in the other," she said, carefully supervising Brian as he tapered the little man's pants so they tucked into his boots. She showed him how to use a V-tool to give texture to the little man's beard, and how to etch around the eyes.

"You can't see his face very well," Brian said.

"In folk art," she said, "you don't have to be exact. Back a hundred years ago they needed simple shapes that could withstand hard use. A father would carve a basic toy like this for his son, and the boy would use his imagination to fill in the details. Even Einstein believed imagination was more important than knowledge."

Brian eyed the wood in his hand. "Someday I'll carve one of these for *my* son."

Annie exchanged a glance with Taylor, and they both looked at the nine-year-old orphan who looked forward to a family of his own someday.

"The hat is kinda big, isn't it?" Brian asked.

"We have to be careful now," Annie pointed out. "The grain takes a turn right there. If we take off too much, the wood may split, so we'll bevel the edge to give the illusion that the brim is thinner than it is."

"Is that one of its quirks?" asked Brian, trying out the new word.

Annie smiled at him. "It is," she replied. "Just one of those surprises that keep things exciting."

"Interesting," said Taylor, catching Annie's attention, "that you would see it that way."

She knew what he was implying. She'd said that he was full of surprises, but with him she was still wary, and they both knew it. She glanced away, unable to meet his gaze.

She gathered up three little axes that Bear had roughed out and laid one beside Brian and one in front of herself. Then she extended one to Taylor. As he reached to take it from her, she looked at him directly. "Perhaps we should bury this."

"The hatchet?" he asked.

"It's time, don't you think?" She paused as he looked into her eyes. She swallowed and took a deep breath, gathering her courage. "I'll try to open my mind, if you'll try to be patient."

His eyes warmed as he plucked the ax from her fingers. "Consider it a deal."

The tension between them eased considerably, and Annie began to enjoy the lesson. She showed them how to drive a hole with a hand drill and how to whittle the ax handle until it could fit securely like a toothpick between the little man's hands.

Brian carefully drilled a hole in the toy's back, and Annie showed him how to bend a nine-inch piece of coat-hanger wire and thread it into the back, then curve it in an arc, and attach a small block of wood to the end. They set the toy on the driftwood log and bent the wire to adjust the pendulum block until they achieved a balance.

With a measure of satisfaction Brian gave his toy a push and watched it rock back and forth, his miniature woodcutter obediently hacking with his ax at the log on which he stood.

"It works," Brian announced with a glow of pride.

Taylor patted his shoulder. "You did it."

Brian looked up at Annie. "Thanks," he said softly.

She ruffled his hair. "Ready for milk and cookies?"

"You bet!" he said, with the gusto that he'd lacked when he'd walked through her door that morning.

She fixed ham sandwiches as well, and carried everything downstairs on a big tray. Meanwhile Brian and Taylor were painting the three toys with oil paints.

"Hey, Annie," Brian called as she approached, "I gave yours a red shirt and blue pants just like Taylor is wearing."

She glanced at Taylor, who looked gorgeous in his red polo shirt and trim blue jeans. "Sounds good to me," she said lightly as she set down the tray.

Brian put aside his painting to dive into lunch. After Taylor finished his sandwich, he wandered around her work area, glancing at the rows of tools in their holders on the pine-plank walls, looking over the progress of her new designs.

He stopped in his tracks when he recognized the photo lying beside a project. It was the color snapshot of the doe and fawn crossing the golf course. He replaced the photo and stared at the work beside it. He could pick out the smooth surface of the putting green and the undulating fairway in front of it. Nearby lay the half-carved form of the doe.

He turned, and when his eyes met hers, she saw the light of recognition in them. "It's coming right along. What are you going to call it?"

"Morning Round," she said simply.

He nodded thoughtfully. "It suits." Though they were ten feet apart, there was the shared intimacy of that mutual memory. "I'd like to see it when you're finished."

She almost said she'd call him, but thought better of it. Between them, things could always change on a moment's notice. Best not to make promises she couldn't keep. "It'll be here," she said finally.

"And will it be for sale?"

"Probably." At this point in her business, she felt that she couldn't hold many pieces back from the market.

"I'd like to have first option"—he turned to gauge her reaction—"if that's all right with you."

"Okay," she said, realizing that she was committing herself to more than she'd intended. However, business was business, as Bear was always reminding her.

"Look at this, Annie," said Brian, holding up the last toy after he'd finished painting it.

She draped her arm across his narrow shoulders as she studied the three woodcutters. "I don't know which I like best. They all look great."

Brian gazed up at her, looking pleased. "I think I still like mine the best."

"Well," she said, "take your pick."

"I get to keep it?" His eyes were wide with hope.

The uncertainty in his rather high-pitched voice made her sad. There had probably been little in Brian's life that he could call his own, so he didn't expect to keep things the way other kids did. "Of course you get to keep it. You made it."

He nodded at the logic of what she'd said. "Then you get to keep yours, and Taylor gets to keep his. Right?"

She smiled down at him. "If Taylor wants his woodcutter, he can take him."

"Well, I should hope so." Taylor put on an expression of mock outrage. "I worked so hard on it while you guys were making all kinds of mistakes on yours."

They laughed at him, and Annie passed the plate of peanut butter cookies. Taylor took one reluctantly. "You can try to silence me with cookies, but we all know the real truth."

Brian giggled. "Yeah, I guess we do."

"Smart aleck," Taylor accused teasingly.

The bell over the door jingled as a couple of customers entered the store. Hearing the sound, Bear entered the shop from his workroom in back.

"Oh, I didn't know if you were here, Annie," he said. "Looks like you've got company—I'll take care of the customers."

Brian's eyes grew round as he looked up at the giant with the full beard and twinkling brown eyes. "Gosh, who's that?" he whispered as Bear showed the ladies to the glass case of miniatures they wanted to see.

"My brother," Annie replied.

Brian looked up at her to be sure she wasn't joking. "Really? He doesn't look like you."

"We had the same daddy, different mothers," she said simply.

Across the table Taylor was taking it all in.

"When you were little, did your brother beat you up?" Brian asked, as if it were the most natural thing in the world for the big to bully the small.

Annie shook her head sadly. "We never met until we were grown up."

"Why?" It was a child's innocent question.

"Well," Annie began slowly, choosing her words as she went, "my father left my mother and me and later met Bear's mother, and they had him. For a long time Bear and I didn't know about each other. When he found out that he had a sister, he looked me up. He kept calling until I agreed to meet him one day, and strangely enough, we became friends." She shrugged. "We've been working together ever since."

"What happened to your dad?" Brian asked.

Annie dropped her eyes. "He died."

Brian looked at her earnestly. "At your brother's house?"

Annie hesitated before shaking her head. "By

that time our father had left Bear's mother and was married to someone else."

Brian nodded sagely. "My daddy did that too. I don't know even where he went." The youngster thought for a moment, then looked at Annie directly. "Are you still mad at him?"

"My dad?" she asked, caught off guard by his unexpected question. She thought about her answer, aware that if she tried to evade the issue, he'd sense it. She knew that kids had a knack for detecting lies. Children's radar was alert to telling pauses and different tones, the subtle nuances. "I was mad at him for a long time," she said honestly, "but I think I'm starting to understand some things. Maybe I can let go and forgive him completely one of these days."

Brian looked at her face and sighed. "Yeah, maybe me too."

The customers filed out with packages under their arms. Bear walked over with a look of satisfaction on his face. "Why is it I can sell your work but not mine?"

She grinned at him. "Well, you're in luck. After you left yesterday, I sold two of your chairs to some college kids for their fraternity house."

"Hey, that'll make you saleswoman of the month," Bear said with a teasing smile. "By the way, who's this good-looking guy?" he said, nodding at Brian. "Not you, ugly," he said, pointing to Taylor, who nodded back goodnaturedly.

Taylor reached across the table to clap Brian's shoulder. "This is my main man, Brian Jones. Meet Bear Malone. This is the man who carves tree trunks with a chainsaw."

Brian's face filled with awe. "Really?"

Bear smiled, and his whole face seemed to light up. "That's what I do."

"Gosh, can I see?" Brian looked to Taylor for approval.

Taylor nodded, and Bear said, "Come along, then."

Brian followed Bear, lengthening his stride, trying to match steps with the big man.

There was an awkward pause as Annie and Taylor glanced at each other. He gave her a wry smile. "Alone at last."

She recognized his attempt to dissipate the tension between them and chuckled softly.

"I have a favor to ask you," he said gently.

She looked up quickly. "Oh?"

"Some of us have organized a charity benefit, a black-tie affair, to raise money for another bus for the Children's Home. There will be a silent auction. A lot of area businesses have donated items for the sale. I was hoping you'd be willing to donate one of your carvings."

She glanced around, wondering what would be appropriate. "Do you have a preference?"

"We'd be glad to have anything you'd give us, and besides, I think it'd be an opportunity for a lot of people to see your work."

"Sounds good. What do you think they'd like?"

He glanced around. "Some of those attending will be wildlife enthusiasts; others will be hunters. I'm sure that any of your decoys would be a hit."

She walked to the decoy display and studied the various carvings. "The pair of mallards?"

He smiled as he looked at the male with his fantastic iridescent green plumage and his mate with her camouflage feathers and dark, gentle eyes. "Very generous of you. I'll make them the featured item of the auction and put a picture of them on the cover of the sales list."

She smiled. "I'd like that."

"Then it's a deal?" He extended his hand, and

she put her hand in his. He gave hers a firm shake and added, "Of course, it would be in your best interest if you attended the auction as well."

"It would?" she asked, casting him a skeptical glance.

"I'm sure meeting you would boost the bids. And the higher the bidding goes, the better it reflects on you."

She could follow his logic, but sensed an ulterior motive tucked in there somewhere. "I see."

"I would be happy to escort you that evening," he continued casually. "There will be a dinner and a dance. I'm sure you'd be more comfortable going with someone you know."

He was still holding her hand. "You think of everything, Mr. Smooth."

He shrugged, as though it were an affliction he couldn't help. "Is that an affirmative, Ms. Malone?"

"When is this little shindig?"

"Next Saturday."

She shrugged. "I think I can make room on my calendar."

"Thank you, Ms. Malone. And the children thank you too."

She sighed disgustedly, half-annoyed that he could manipulate her with such ease. "You rotten—"

"Now, now," he interrupted, "no more endearments. There's a child in the next room, you know."

"Then a display of affection such as this"—she withdrew her hand from his—"would be inappropriate as well."

"I wouldn't be so sure."

He caught her wrist and drew her to him with more momentum than he'd intended. She collided with his chest, her breath releasing in a whoosh. Their faces only inches apart, she looked directly up into his eyes and lost herself in those dark pools of blue. She wanted to object, but couldn't find her voice.

Slowly he lowered his mouth to hers and kissed her the way he'd wanted to all morning, leisurely, thoroughly. He held her tightly, wanting to drive out the doubts that made her keep resisting him, accusing him, and distrusting him.

A moment later she pushed away from him and glanced guiltily over her shoulder toward Bear's workshop. Brian's voice came to her. Though she couldn't understand his words, his tone told her that he was still enthralled with whatever Bear was showing him.

She turned away and raked her fingers through her hair, trying to get a grip on her emotions. Taylor started to reach out to her when Brian came scampering back into the room.

"Taylor!" the boy exclaimed. "Bear wants to give me this." He held up a chunk of log a foot long. On the front side was a carving of an Indian's face, an arresting face filled with pride and strength. Brian turned the piece in his hands to show that on the back the bark still remained. "Can I keep it, huh?"

"If Bear doesn't mind," Taylor said with an indulgent smile.

"Oh boy!" Brian grinned. "I want to come back next Saturday."

"You and the boys are going on a fishing trip with the city councilmen next Saturday, remember?"

"Oh." The child's face clouded with the confusing prospect of wanting to do two things but only having time for one. His face brightened. "Maybe the next Saturday I can come back?"

"That's the weekend we're going on a trail ride."

The boy's eyes widened as a thought occurred. "I know . . . Annie can go with us. The other guys like her too." Impulsively, he slipped his hand into hers and looked up with a guileless, hopeful expression. "You want to go with us, don't you?"

"Well . . . of course, I do, but—"

Brian's forehead wrinkled as he heard an excuse in the making. "Taylor wants you to come too." He looked at Taylor and nodded to prompt some support.

"I think it's a great idea." Taylor crossed his arms and looked at Annie with an expression that asked her how she was going to get out of this one.

Brian tapped Annie's shoulder. "We're going way up in the mountains where you can see all this neat stuff. It's going to be really cool. Please?"

Her shoulders sagged in defeat. She couldn't find it in her heart to disappoint Brian. "Okay."

"Great!" The boy hugged her arm.

The look in Taylor's eyes told her that Brian wasn't the only one who was pleased.

Ten

Annie looked into the full-length mirror on the back of her bedroom door and surveyed herself with a critical eye. The black cocktail dress had set her budget back a mile, but its lines were classic, and once again she told herself that she'd be able to wear it on other occasions—even if she had bought the outfit with nothing but Taylor McQuaid's reaction in mind.

Even the barely black hose and the black suede pumps she was wearing and the simple envelope evening bag in her hand were chosen to please his taste as much as hers.

She fluffed her hair that framed her face like a cloud, wondering why she'd treated herself to a salon conditioning and hairstyling. She sighed as she closed her bedroom door and walked into the living room to check the clock.

Why in the world had she commited herself to not just one date with Taylor McQuaid but two? Tonight the dinner dance and silent auction, next weekend a trail ride through the mountains. Could they date and still maintain a lasting friendship? Annie fervently hoped so.

She answered her door after his second knock. For a few seconds she could only stand in her doorway speechless at the stunning figure he cut in his black tuxedo. The white collar set off his healthy tan, highlighted his toothpaste-ad smile, and deepened the blue of his bedroom eyes, which filled with appreciation as he looked her up and down.

His words came slowly. "You look beautiful, Annie." He wasn't tossing off compliments automatically. The way he'd said it made it sound sincere.

"Thank you." *I could say the same about you,* she thought but left the words unsaid. As she stepped back to let him in, he handed her a box containing a white orchid. After he pinned it to her dress a moment later, he couldn't resist stealing a quick kiss, and she couldn't resist letting him.

After a twenty-minute drive they arrived at their destination. An attendant opened her car door, then a valet whisked away Taylor's car. Annie was struck by the timeless elegance as Taylor escorted her inside the Broadmoor, one of the nation's oldest country-club resorts, nestled at the foothills of the Rockies.

The ballroom was already filled with formally attired people who sipped champagne as they strolled around tables to view the items on exhibit. They busily filled out slips of paper that they dropped into black silk tophats to make their silent bids. Annie was amazed by the variety of items donated to the auction and pleased by the prominent placement of her hand-carved mallards.

Just as he'd promised, Taylor had made them the featured object of the auction. A color picture of the ducks graced the cover of the sales list, and they were the first item listed inside, with a nice description of her work and the location of her shop.

The white-covered round table holding her pair of mallards was in the center of the room. Annie would have preferred to watch from a distance, but Taylor led her to the heart of the action and introduced her to the interested bidders surrounding the table.

Many seemed genuinely delighted to meet her, commenting with enthusiasm on the realistic detail of her decoys. Bidding slips continued to fill the inverted top-hat positioned beside the mallards.

"Young lady," one silver-haired gentleman addressed her, "if my bid doesn't win that lovely pair of decoys, I want to commission you to carve and paint another pair just for me."

"I would be happy to," Annie replied.

Five more orders for decoys rolled in, two of them with suggestions for new poses.

"Actually wood ducks are my favorite. They're the most colorful," a young man beside her said. He wore his blond hair long, and a large diamond twinkled in one ear. The look in his eyes as he gazed at her held admiration for more than the beauty of her carvings. "Do you have wood ducks in your collection?"

She nodded. "There's a pair of them in the window of our shop."

"I'll be sure to stop by," he said, moving closer until Taylor casually stepped between them.

"There are some people I want you to meet," Taylor said, guiding her away. When they were out of earshot, he bent to her ear. "You have to be careful at these things. Some people drink too much, and others are always on the make."

"You don't say?" she said, a wry mockery in her voice as she slanted a look up at him.

Taylor seated her at the head table beside himself and introduced her to the others there. The meal was delicious, and the company around them friendly. Annie had always assumed that these society types would be cool and snobbish to someone like her, but they seemed to accept her easily, some actually in awe of her talent.

After dinner Taylor led her to the dance floor. The lights were dim where she turned, and he gathered her close into his arms. Her hand rested upon his shoulder. Beneath the rich fabric of his tux, she could feel the strong ridge of muscles. Her temple touched his jaw, and she inhaled the enticing scent of his cologne. His breathing came to her ears more clearly than the bluesy notes from the musicians playing in the corner.

Their feet barely shifted, but her thighs tingled where they brushed against his. Warmth sought warmth as her pliant curves nestled against his muscled angles. Nestling her head at the base of his throat, she listened to his pulse race against her ear. Somehow they fit perfectly together, their dancing a tender embrace set to music.

The lights came up as the master of ceremonies tapped on the microphone for attention. Taylor took Annie's hand, and they stepped apart.

"If I may have your attention, ladies and gentlemen . . . the results of the silent auction have been tabulated, and I am ready to announced the new owners of the wonderful items auctioned off this evening. It is also my pleasure to announced that the proceeds of the auction have topped the figure raised last year, so the Children's Home will indeed have that new bus right away!"

There was a round of applause, and then the announcer moved to the list of winning bidders.

Annie's carvings went to the silver-haired gentleman who'd praised her work just a few hours ago. She scanned the room and saw him standing beside the pair of mallards. With a smile he raised his glass to her. The look of pleasure on his face was all the thanks she needed.

The evening came to a close as people gathered their new acquisitions and wrote their checks. Dozens of new fans took down the name of her shop and its address. Just as Taylor had predicted, the evening brought her work more exposure than weeks of advertising.

"It will be months before I can fill the specialty orders I received this evening," she told Taylor on the drive home.

"Well, I hope you'll still have time for me."

She paused a moment as his meaning sank in. He'd never mentioned a future for them. Each time they'd seen each other, it had always seemed that it could be the last time.

He downshifted and glanced at her, his brows raised in question. A smile softened her lips. "I think I could squeeze you in."

The corners of his mouth lifted. "Glad to hear it."

"I didn't see Nathan Patrari tonight," she said casually.

He accelerated through a curve before responding. "Mr. Patrari didn't receive an invitation this year."

"Was that your doing?"

He chuckled. "Crossed him off my Christmas list too."

"My, my, you are ruthless."

"I hope you know by now that I'm not like him." The look on his face grew serious.

"I think I've learned that much."

He nodded his satisfaction. "You know, the long-haired dude you were visiting with this evening is enough like Patrari to be his brother."

"Oh?"

"A rich kid playing at being a rock star."

Annie could sense a note of jealousy in him, and found it oddly comforting. "Then I suppose he doesn't need another groupie."

Taylor nodded. "I'm glad you realize that." His shoulders dropped as the tension in him seem to disappear.

He *is* jealous, Annie thought to herself, and a bubble of hope seemed to blossom inside her.

Back at her apartment Taylor leaned against the doorjamb as she turned the key in the lock. "Gosh, I could use a cup of coffee." He yawned and patted his mouth. "I'd hate to drive all the way home nodding off like this."

Annie swung the door open and gestured for him to enter. "I can take a hint."

"Thanks," he said as he breezed past her," don't mind if I do."

"You're impossible," she teased as she followed him in and flicked on the light.

"Keep it up," he said, playfully shaking his finger at her, "and I might not leave."

"Oh, yes you will," she called out in a singsong voice from the kitchen, "or I'll call my brother. . . ."

Taylor cleared his throat, sobering. "Now you're not playing fair. . . ."

Neither are you, Annie thought, as she glanced his way and plugged in the coffeemaker. Being alone with Taylor McQuaid had become a dangerous situation for her. Being in his arms seemed to sabotage her self-control. *I'll be strong,* she promised herself, but wondered for how long.

While she puttered in the kitchen, Taylor wandered around her apartment. He was hoping to find the completed project she called Morning

Round, but it wasn't there. Instead he found a carving he had never seen before.

Atop a bookcase on the far wall, he took down the small carving. It was shaped like a man's head, and it fit into the palm of his hand. He stared into the face for an instant before he recognized it as his own.

There was a rattle of cup in a saucer behind him, and he turned. She glanced at the carving in his hand, and their eyes met and held for a moment before she broke eye contact and bent to set the two saucers on her coffee table.

She tried to swallow, but her heart was in her throat, her pulse hammering behind her eyes. She should never have left that carving where he could find it. She should have known that leaving it in an out-of-the-way place was risky. Now he'd found it, and what was he going to think? She felt awkward . . . exposed . . . and vulnerable while he held her carving of him in his hand.

She wondered if her feelings toward him were easily readable in her work. Could he see how much she'd come to admire him? Could he tell by the time she'd obviously spent carving it how often he'd been on her mind? Would he know by the accuracy of every detail how well she had memorized his face?

She had etched the character that she'd come to recognize in his high cheekbones, his firm nose, his strong jaw. She'd caught the sincerity in his straightforward gaze. His serious side she'd captured in the lines above his brow, his playful side in the lift at the corners of his mouth. It was all there in wood for anyone to see, stained a dark teak like his tan—and the last person in the world she'd wanted to see that piece had been Taylor himself.

Because her knees were growing weak and because she was hoping to change the subject abruptly, she sank to the sofa and fixed her gaze on the front door across the room. Her body tensed as she felt him sit down beside her. He moved his hand so that the carving of himself was just below her gaze. Her eyes betrayed her as she glanced down.

"Does he have a name?" Taylor asked in a low voice.

She let out a long sigh and looked at him and then back to the lump of wood in his palm. "When I started it, my intention was to call it 'A Study in Arrogance'"—she paused for an instant to summon her courage—"but I know now that title is not appropriate."

Taylor rotated the face he was holding in his hand. "You don't think he looks so arrogant anymore?"

She shook her head. "As it came to life in my hands"—her gaze dropped away—"and as I got to know my subject better . . . I realized that arrogance was not the trait I was trying to capture."

"And what trait did you find instead?" he asked softly.

She looked at him, and there was confusion in her eyes. "I think I'm still trying to sort that out."

He carefully placed the carving on the table and reached out to cup her chin in his palm. Turning her face to his, he let his gaze study her eyes, the green eyes that haunted his visions at night and filled his daydreams. His gaze roamed over her face, a face that he'd thought was gorgeous the moment he'd first seen her, a face that had come to mean so much more to him since then. Slowly he brought his mouth to hers. His lips grazed hers tentatively, tasting, memorizing.

She sat very still, soaking up the sensations of

his touch. The care he took to savor her lips made it impossible for her to move. She felt totally vulnerable and open to him. He could taste the emotion on her lips as easily as he could read the feelings carved into her work. He knew what she knew. They needed no words, only touch.

Gently, he took her into his arms and held her, stroking her hair, letting his fingertips stroke down her back where her dress draped low. Her head lay beneath his chin, her face against his lapel.

Slowly Annie raised herself up and looked into his eyes. Somehow she'd had a premonition on the first evening that he'd walked into her place that this moment would be inevitable. Somewhere along the way she'd fallen in love with Taylor McQuaid. It was a fact that she had been able to distrust, deny, and ignore—until he had discovered it. When he'd looked at her carving of him, he had known. Now there was no use hiding her love for him, and so, with a sigh of resignation, she accepted it.

Perhaps he was the rogue she'd always suspected, or perhaps he wasn't. It didn't matter anymore. What did matter was how she felt, and for the first time in a long time, she was going to act on her feelings alone. The world never offered any guarantees, though she'd always wished otherwise. There might never be another night with him, but at least she would have the memory of this night to hold in her heart forever.

She reached up and drew on one end of his tie until the bow unraveled and fell away. He remained still, his eyes on hers as she unbuttoned his top shirt button and then, one by one, the rest of them.

This was her move, and after waiting so long for

it, he was more than a little surprised at what was happening. He'd hoped for weeks that she would grow fond of him, forget the image of Mr. Smooth that always seemed to obstruct her vision and come to know *him* and care for *him*, the way he had grown to care for her.

So many times he'd wanted to rush her along, but he'd forced himself to be patient. Long ago he'd realized that this decision had to be hers, or there would be regrets. And the last thing he wanted to see in her eyes tomorrow was remorse.

Rising slowly to her feet, she took his hand. Without a word she led him to her bedroom door. She gave the door a push and it swung open. Moonlight streaming through lace curtains illuminated the white quilt on the old four-poster bed.

She glanced up at him as they stood in the open doorway. This was a small, modest room filled with simple things. No heart-shaped mattresses here, no silk sheets, no Jacuzzi, no lighted candles— none of the things he'd surely experienced before. How would anything she could offer possibly compare to the romantic interludes that the jet set reportedly enjoyed?

"It's not fancy," she said.

"*Where* does *not* matter."

"But the *who* is important, isn't it?" she said, seeking a little reassurance. Despite her feelings for him, she didn't want to be just another notch on his bedpost, just another name in his little black book.

"Oh, yes," he agreed huskily, "*who* is important, and *when.* . . ."

It was then that she realized just how much restraint he'd shown her, on so many occasions . . . even in the honeymoon suite.

"The *when* seems inevitable," she whispered, "but the *why* has to matter too."

"Why?" he repeated, looking into her eyes. "Because it's meant to be."

The look of love in his eyes was enough. She gave herself over to the desire she'd held back for so long as she wrapped her arms around his neck. Plunging her fingers into his thick hair, she decided to indulge her every fantasy. Tonight there would be no holding back.

He let himself follow his instincts and do what he'd wanted to do the first night he'd visited her at her apartment; he scooped her into his arms and carried her to bed.

There he would take his time; he would spoil her. He would take care to show her that she was special to him. He removed her shoes one at a time, then he slid his fingers over her ankles and stroked her shapely calves. Massaging behind her knees, his fingers lingered at her hemline as he looked into her eyes. She lay fully stretched out, her head upon her pillow, her hair fanned out around her face.

His long fingers disappeared beneath her dress, and he watched the corners of her mouth lift as he stroked her firm thighs. He released one nylon and drew it slowly down her leg, letting his fingertips trail over her smooth, silky skin. He tossed the stocking into the air and reached for the second one as the first floated through the air.

As he sat upon the bed beside her, she sat up and kissed him. Gently he trailed butterfly kisses down her throat as he slid the straps of her gown off her shoulders. His fingers found the zipper on the side and pulled it down. The dress fell in folds to her lap. She lay back, and he drew it over her hips and down her legs.

In the moonlight he gazed at her, clad only in the

black lace underthings she'd selected with him in mind. "Oh, Annie," he said, his voice husky with appreciation.

She sat up to face him. "My turn," she said, reaching to the side of the bed to slip off his shoes and socks. Catching her lower lip between her teeth, she slid her fingers inside his open shirt and pushed it back over his shoulders. Her fingers trembled slightly as they moved his belt through the buckle. She unhooked his pants and took a deep breath as she slid down the zipper.

He tossed his shirt aside as he got to his feet to stand beside the bed. Her heart was pounding in her ears as she hooked her thumbs inside his waistband. Drawing down his trousers and briefs, she heard his soft groan as her hands found him and stroked intimately. Again, she realized the degree of his control as he'd let her choose her way slowly.

She rose to her knees, caressing him with her sensitive fingers. He cupped her face in his hands and brought his mouth to hers eagerly. As their kisses deepened, his fingers nimbly removed the last wisps of lace from her body and stroked the places they had covered, teasing, tantalizing, filling her every pore with a white-hot desire as he pleasured her.

With her name on his lips, he eased down beside her on the bed, where he worshiped her with his mouth and his hands, showing her what was in his heart. Their legs entwined, and he rolled to brace himself above her. Her eyes darkened as she reached for him. Kissing his lips, she guided him home inside her. Then began the timeless rhythm that stoked their fires while it fed them.

They topped one summit after another until it seemed their pleasure could not increase. Then, suddenly, something bloomed inside them and tipped them over the edge.

Later she lay in his arms, her body soft with satisfaction, her heart filled with contentment. Never had she imagined that he would be such a tender lover, never had she thought he would so cherish her with his hands, his body, and his soft words while he pushed her to peak after peak.

When she had first met him, she'd assumed that, like most playboys, he would be preoccupied with his own needs. As she'd got to know him better, she'd realized that he was in many ways an unselfish man; but only in the past hour had she discovered just how giving he could be.

Today her heart was full of admiration as well as love for him. It would be difficult to give him up, and impossible to forget him. He had spoiled her to the point that no one else would ever measure up. It made her sad to contemplate his eventual absence, and she pushed the thought aside in her struggle to live this one day, to enjoy this time with him, to let happen what would happen.

"Wake up, lazybones," he whispered as he kissed her eyelids.

"I'm awake," she said dreamily.

He took her into his arms and kissed her until she was wide awake.

"Why did you do that?" she asked.

"Do what?" He paused to look into her eyes.

"Make me all hungry again, just when I was feeling so satisfied."

"You were, huh?" The expression on his face reflected masculine pride. "Well, now that I've started something, I'll bet you're going to expect me to finish it too."

"You got it." She settled cozily into his arms.

He sighed. "A man's work is never done."

"Yeah, never." She reached for a pillow to swat

him, but as he kissed her fervently, her arm paused in midair and changed course to wrap around him.

It was midmorning when he finally dragged her into the shower. His lovemaking had left her feeling drowsy and lazy. "Hurry up, woman," he prodded her affectionately. "We've got a drive ahead of us."

"What?"

He turned on the spray over her head, lathered his hands, and began to work his fingers over her back. "Ohh," she moaned gratefully. "I'll give you ten minutes to stop that."

He chuckled. "Okay, but then you throw on some jeans and head to the car."

"Why?"

"Because we're going to grab some brunch and head to the mountains, so bring your camera."

She turned to face him. "Do I have any input in these plans?"

His hands began to work suds in small circles from her shoulders downward, as they had over her back. "Input?" he asked as his hands worked lower. "Sure, you can have input. What did you want to suggest?"

She closed her eyes and swallowed against the urges he was bringing to the surface again. "I don't remember."

"What am I going to do with you?"

She shrugged. "You'll think of something, I'm sure."

An hour later they were outdoors in the crisp chill of an early November morning. They climbed into his car and rode a few blocks to a restaurant. After a brunch buffet he drove them into the mountains. Annie settled her camera case between her feet and leaned back to enjoy the scenery. Awhile later they turned onto a private road and wound through a forest of aspen, pine, spruce, and larch, where fallen leaves and pine needles carpeted the forest floor.

Taylor slowed as they approached a rustic log lodge with a huge covered porch that overlooked a breathtaking mountain view. Reaching into his glove box, he pressed a remote button, and the garage door rose. He pulled his car inside and dropped the door.

"Wait here while I get the light." He climbed out and flipped a switch before coming to her door.

With an air of unmistakable pride he led her upstairs and inside. "This is home."

She turned a slow circle in the open room, glancing at the tall windows toward the view and the huge stone fireplace that covered one wall. "I like it," she said, moving to the long mantel over the fireplace. Her lips curved in a smile as she spotted the woodchopper toy he'd carved the day that he'd brought Brian to her shop. She gave the toy a gentle push, and the little woodsman rocked up and down on the mantel.

"Be right back," he said, moving toward the door. "Gotta unload the car."

She nodded absently as she walked toward the end of the mantel to look at a cluster of framed photographs. In them she saw a much younger Taylor standing with an older man beside a half-assembled jalopy. The older man resembled Taylor so closely, he had to be his father. There was another picture of them, this time with a woman standing on the front steps of a small white bungalow. Behind them a pine-cone Christmas wreath was hanging on the door.

Their arms were looped together, and their smiles were similar. On the faces of all three was the glow of close family unity. The woman was wearing a modest housecoat, the man was dressed in dark-blue work clothes, and a young Taylor was wearing jeans and a plaid shirt. They all looked happy, but something didn't jibe.

This wasn't the columned mannor house where she'd imagined he'd grown up. The house in the photo could have been in many places in and around Colorado Springs, but she was sure that it wasn't in an exclusive neighborhood or lining a golf course.

She caught a glimpse of Taylor carrying a grocery bag into the kitchen. A moment later he walked to the fireplace with a large cardboard box tucked under one arm.

"What's that?" she asked.

"You'll see." He stopped to light the paper and kindling already in place under a stack of logs on the grate. When the flames were crackling, he turned his attention to the cardboard box. He opened and unpacked it with care.

Annie's mouth fell open as the pair of carved mallards emerged from the box. "How did you get those? I thought that older gentleman, Mr. Martin, won that bid at the auction."

He smiled as he placed them on his mantel. "He did."

"Then how did you get them?"

"I made him an offer—"

"—that he couldn't refuse," she finished.

"Actually, no. Mr. Martin is a kind man with a sentimental streak. When I explained that these carvings held a special meaning for me, he offered to let me take them for the price of his bid."

She blinked in confusion. "You could have bought another pair for less at our shop."

"Wouldn't have been the same. These carvings

will always remind me of the day that you donated them, of the auction . . . of you."

Her smiled was tender. "You're the sentimental one."

"Guilty as charged." He raised his palms. "In any event, Mr. Martin will be around next week to pick out another pair of decoys. He really admires your work. Lots of people do. In fact I wouldn't be surprised if next week isn't pretty busy at your shop."

"Of course you wouldn't have anything to do with that." She gave him a sly smile.

"Like I said, the auction gave your work some exposure. You're the one who gives your work such quality."

"You never told me that before." She took a step toward him.

"I didn't?" He gathered her close in his arms.

"Not the part about the quality."

"I've always believed you're a woman of quality, Annie, but I guess there are still some things about me you're not sure of."

"Correction—there are still some things about you I don't know."

He studied her for a moment. "Do you still think of me as a spoiled playboy on the make?"

She shook her head. "That wasn't fair, was it?"

He shrugged. "Birds-of-a-feather philosophy . . . I suppose."

"Still unfair. Not everyone chooses friends who are carbon copies of themselves." She had learned that much over the last few weeks. "I made some snap judgments about you, Taylor, and I apologize. I suppose that reveals more about my insecurities than anything else."

"That's a lot for anyone to admit." He kissed the tip of her nose. "Apology accepted." He kissed her lips. "By the way, apologies always make me hungry. Could I interest you in a glass of wine, a tour, and a plate of Chicken Malone?"

"Who's doing the cookin'?" she asked.

"We are."

"Cookin' up trouble again, huh?"

"Not if I have anything to say about it."

"Then you're on."

He led her to the kitchen, where he uncorked a chilled bottle of Piesporter and filled two glasses. Annie followed him through the tour and back to the fireplace.

"I love the layout," she said, "and the view from every room is spectacular."

"I drew the plans for it and watched it go up. I keep an apartment in the city, but this is my home."

She pointed to the picture of Taylor beside a torn-down jalopy. "I guess you always liked cars."

"Yep—always. Dad and I would find an old nine-fourteen somewhere, rebuild it on the weekends, and sell it for a profit. Everybody wanted a Porsche, and that model was fun and affordable. The one in the picture was a real junker when we found it." He smiled a little. "Going through the gears was like stirring mashed potatoes, but we got it right before we sold it."

"So you weren't born into the family's luxury-car agency?"

He shook his head. "When I was still at the university, I inherited a small sum from an insurance policy and after graduation started a used-car lot. One thing led to another over the years, and eventually I was in a position to buy the agency. So, no, I wasn't born with a silver spoon in my mouth, if that's what you thought."

It was, but she didn't have to say it. It had been obvious all along. She reached for another photo on the mantel, the one of the trio. "Is this your family?"

He nodded, his expression growing somber. "Was my family."

"Oh." Her face fell, "I'm sorry, Taylor."

He shook his head as he glanced at the photo. "It happened a long time ago . . . while I was still in college at Boulder. Every autumn the folks loved to go to my uncle's cabin up in Woodland Hills. One weekend they were on the road back when an early blizzard hit." His features tensed with regret. "They should have pulled off and spent the night, but my dad never thought he could miss a day of work at the factory. The accident report said he skidded into the path of a semi." Taylor swallowed as he glanced away. "At least it was quick. I was told they didn't suffer."

Her fingers closed over his arm. "You really mustn't blame yourself for what happened. It was an accident."

He glanced at her in surprise. "You are perceptive. But think about it, Annie—if I had come home that weekend, I would have driven them, and I would have insisted that we pull off that day."

She shook her head and shrugged. "Who knows? Maybe nothing would have changed. You can't know what was in your father's mind that day. You only think you know the reasons for what he did. And you mustn't blame yourself. They wouldn't want you to do that."

"No . . . they wouldn't." He touched her face, and his expression turned pensive. "I guess the trick is to learn how to forgive."

She nodded.

"Have you learned how to do that, Annie?" His thumb brushed back and forth over her chin.

"What?" Her expression grew wary.

"Have you learned how to forgive . . . your father . . . and yourself?"

Her gaze dropped away, and she took a deep breath. "No, I can't say that I have, actually."

"Well, when you do, let me know."

She could only nod, and hope he'd continue to be patient with her.

Eleven

The next morning Annie shut the door to her apartment and stepped into the sunshine on the open landing. She shivered in the late-autumn chill as she gazed at the mountains in the distance, remembering the thrill of standing beside Taylor on the porch of his lodge the day before.

They had looked down into the deep blue of a glacial-fed lake when the wind had suddenly whipped through the pass and churned the mirror-smooth stillness into the whitecaps of an inland sea.

She thought of Taylor McQuaid, his strength and his gentleness, and realized that she thought of little else these days. But she still had a business to run. Time to get to it, she thought as she started down the steps to the back door of the shop.

"Hello there, stranger," Bear called when he spotted her.

"Let me get that for you." She hopped over the last two steps to hold the door for him as he carried in a box of wood samples left by UPS.

He grunted as he deposited the bulky load atop his work table. Grabbing a curved knife, he slit open the wrapping tape.

"Haven't seen much of you lately." He glanced at her as he opened the box flaps, noting the bright glow in her eyes and the flush in her cheeks. "Have a good weekend?"

"Great." Her smile was warm. "Did you?"

"Yep. Opened the shop for a few hours yesterday afternoon. Did a bang-up business too. Lots of people who'd attended that silent auction had good things to say about you."

"I had a good time. The mallards we donated brought a gratifying price."

"I heard. Good advertising. Brought in a bunch of new customers—the ones with bucks to spend. How's that little guy, Brian?" he asked.

"Haven't seen him lately, but I'll be with him on the trail ride next weekend."

"Well, then I guess I can ask about the big guy . . . Taylor, is it?"

"Fine." She busied herself, helping him unload the samples of wood and laying them out on the table.

"You two getting to be a regular thing now?" His tone was casual, but his eyes were alert as he watched for her reply.

She shrugged. "Hard to say . . . Maybe."

He smiled at her in a way that said he knew her better than that. "Well, it's about time."

She raised her hands to slow him down. "Okay. I'm seeing him . . . for now. I'm probably letting myself in for a big letdown."

"The optimists won't let you into their club with that attitude." There was a teasing light in his dark eyes.

"You should know." She shook her head. "You're the incurable optimist of the decade."

"Well—no guts, no glory." He grinned at her.

"Yeah, remind me of that after I crash and burn, will you?" She set the box aside.

His look softened. "Really, Annie, it's time to start livin', time to take some risks. You're too young to be so cautious' and *conventional.* Let a little excitement into your life."

"I'm getting my share of excitement, thank you."

"Really?" His eyes took on a lecherous gleam. "Hmmm, tell me more."

"Chill out. I'm not divulging details."

He scratched his beard as his expression grew puzzled. "Well, forgive me for being dense, but I don't get it."

"Get what?"

"If you really like this guy, why the forecast of gloom and doom?"

She shrugged and avoided eye contact. "It's just the kind of guy he is, I guess." She stopped moving and slapped her hands on the table. "Okay, granted he's not the spoiled, got-it-handed-to-you-on-a-silver-platter kid I thought he was, but he's still so handsome and so charming . . ."

"So? Isn't that what every woman wants?"

"That's my point. I ask you, how can a guy like that settle for one woman? He's going to attract women all his life—a lot of temptation, I'd say." Doubt clouded her eyes, and a look of hurt passed over her features.

Bear shook his head. "You're getting things confused, Sis."

"I'm just afraid that . . ."

"Fears aren't so big once you say them aloud." Bear raised his brows quizzically.

"Well, when a man is handsome and charming and rich like Taylor . . ."

"Yes," Bear prompted.

"What's to keep him from turning out like our

father? A man who couldn't stay with one woman, a man who was in love with the jet-set lifestyle . . . ?"

Bear shook his head. "You're only checking the stats, Sis, looking only at the surface of it. Our dad and Taylor McQuaid aren't cut from the same cloth."

"How can you be so sure?" She paused, looking at him.

He picked up two lengths of wood. "Take these samples, for instance. They look alike, don't they? Same color, same variety, same texture."

She nodded.

"But that's where their similarities end." He turned the two blocks of wood, examining them carefully. He handed her one of them. "Check the small knot on the upper end there."

She found it and rubbed her fingers over it.

"Structural weakness. Most likely will split there when we stress it. Now check this one out." He handed her the other sample.

She turned it in her hands, smoothing it with her fingertips, looking at it critically. She glanced up with a question in her eyes.

"Good stuff," he replied. "Should stand up under stress and last over the course of time."

She set the wood down. "Your point?"

"Don't lump people together like you do." He shook his head. "Everybody's different in little ways that make a big difference."

"But how can you be sure you pick the right one?" Her hand came to rest on the wood without the blemish.

"Same way we select wood. Experience. No substitute for it."

She gave him a wry smile. "Experience can be painful—who knows, maybe fatal."

"If worse comes to worst, you'll survive. You survived a difficult childhood, didn't you?"

She nodded. "We both did."

"I think that's part of the problem, if you ask me." He shrugged. "I know, I know, you didn't ask me. But, honey, you gotta quit comparing every good-lookin', smooth-talkin' guy you meet to our father. Face it, he was fickle. That was his critical flaw. Not every good-lookin', charming lad is gonna turn out to be like him." He grinned at her. "Take me, for example."

She chuckled. "I get the point." She walked around the table and hugged his arm. "I hope you're right, big brother, I really do."

A moment later, she lifted her head and looked up at him quizzically. "You always make me feel better."

He hugged her. "I'm glad to hear it."

"I'm not so resentful of Dad. Maybe his weaknesses were structural, like you say." She glanced at the wood sample with the flaws. "Maybe, to a large extent, he couldn't help himself . . . he was just weak." It occurred to her that *weak* was not a word she would ever use to describe Taylor Mc-Quaid.

"I think you've got that right." He wrapped his arm around his sister. "Dad was weak and addicted to more things than we'll ever know."

Her eyes filled with tears. "Maybe it *is* time for me to forgive and forget where he's concerned."

"You'll be happier when you do. I know I am." He gave her shoulders a squeeze. "He had good intentions, you know, but he fell far short of following them through. I think he loved us both, but he couldn't face us because then he'd have to face himself too."

She nodded, and the tears welling in her eyes spilled over and coursed down her cheeks. She usually cried alone in the privacy of her room, but in Bear's arms she opened the floodgates and released the hurt she'd harbored for a lifetime.

When her emotions were spent, she felt ten pounds lighter. She'd finally forgiven the father who'd hurt her so long ago, and in doing so, she'd begun to tear down the walls that separated her from the others in her life.

"I'm okay now." She lifted her head and tried to muster a watery smile for the brother who had come through for her again.

He patted the top of her head. "You're such a hard head, but I figured you'd come around one of these days."

He grinned at her, and she reared back to swat him. "That's right," she accused, "give me a hard time."

"What's a brother for?"

She swiped at the moisture on her face with the backs of her hands and moved to a mirror to repair the damage.

The bell tinkled over the front door to the shop. "Well," Bear said, "sounds like more customers walking through our door. New orders been flooding in since the charity benefit. Business used to be a little slow. . . . Say, Annie, would you like me to cover the shop for a while?"

Annie fluffed her hair and sighed in relief. When she turned to face him, there was a new strength in her eyes. "I can handle it. You can stay here. Thanks." She shrugged and turned to walk into the shop to greet the next customer.

"Annie, darling, I'm so glad you're here." Nina reached out to grasp Annie's shoulders to give her a peck on the cheek.

Annie was a bit startled by the warm reception, since she and Nina weren't really that well acquainted.

"I was in here yesterday, and I want you to know that I love your little shop." Nina strolled around the displays and pointed to the corner. "And your studio?"

Annie nodded. "How are the miniatures doing?"

"I'm sold out, dear. That's why I'm here. Since the charity-dinner auction, it seems there's a flurry of interest in your work." She walked to the front, where she gazed at the decoy collection in the window. "My, my, they are lovely. All I've heard about for days was the price your carvings brought at the auction."

Nina picked up a decoy and handed it to Annie. "I'll take this one and its mate. I'm stocking up on Malone carvings."

Annie carried the decoys back to the counter.

"Of course," Nina continued, "the grapevine is buzzing about your becoming McQuaid's new lady."

Annie gave a noncommittal shrug. "That's the thing about rumors: They're so rarely true."

"Ahh, you're so right." Nina paused to stroke the back of one wooden decoy. "Of course, there's usually a grain of truth wedged in there somewhere."

"Is there something else I can do for you?" Annie asked in what she hoped was a pleasant tone.

"Yes! Box up another order of miniatures and throw in a dozen of those darling wood toys. Mrs. Eagleston would love those in the nursery I'm doing for her new grandbaby."

Annie moved behind the counter and opened the glass case to select an assortment of miniatures.

Nina walked to the front of the glass case. "I'll take four of those, four of those, and a half dozen of each of those. Strike while the iron is hot, I always say." Nina gave her a sly smile. "Look, dear, a word to the wise, okay? You are McQuaid's latest and greatest. Enjoy it! Everybody knows he can treat a girl like a queen: wine her, dine her, take her to the mountains, take her on business trips. Okay, so what if it doesn't last forever? What does?"

"I suppose," Bear said in a rumbling voice from behind them, "you'll be needing this."

Annie turned to see him standing in the doorway holding out the box that had held the wood samples. "Thanks," she said, taking it from him.

He gave Annie a look that asked her if she was okay. She figured that he had overheard her exchange with Nina and gave him a slight nod. He stepped to her side and began wrapping the miniatures in tissue paper as Annie lined the box with paper.

Nina scanned the bill and wrote out a check. When Bear had left, she said to Annie contritely, "Listen, Annie, I hope I didn't upset you. People are always going to talk about someone as exciting as Taylor McQuaid. But sometimes my mouth gets to flapping, and I don't know when to stop."

Annie shrugged it off, but when Nina had gone, she frowned pensively.

The week flew by. Taylor took Annie to dinner several times, and they cooked together a few evenings. She had put Nina's gossipy remarks aside. Bear had told her to consider the source, and she knew well enough that rumors were best ignored.

Early the following Saturday Taylor picked her up in the agency van before stopping at the Children's Home. There six eager youngsters, four of them of Indian descent, piled into the back. Brian made sure he was sitting as close to Annie as possible.

The boys seemed to enjoy the drive to Vail, especially when Taylor pointed out a small herd of bighorn sheep grazing along the interstate. When they got to town, Taylor asked, "Want to eat here, boys, or get something to go for a picnic later?" He winked at Annie.

Eager to get to the horses, everyone opted for the picnic. Taylor pulled through a drive-through and picked up a couple of buckets of fried chicken, fries, and several liters of soda.

As they headed for the corral, Brian reached between Annie and Taylor to point his finger at a large hotel just ahead. "That one's pretty," he said.

"Yes, indeed," Taylor agreed quietly.

Annie and Taylor exchanged a meaningful look. Brian was pointing at the Raphael, where they'd shared the honeymoon suite only a few weeks ago.

Ten minutes later the boys were scrambling around inside a corral, selecting their mounts from the eight well-trained horses standing patiently tied to posts, already saddled and bridled.

Taylor made the introductions "Annie, I'd like you to meet Quent Hale, the owner and manager of this trail-riding operation. Quent, this is my friend Annie Malone."

They shook hands. "You have a nice string, Mr. Hale," Annie said, looking at the sleek, well-rounded horses tied to the fence.

Quent shifted his toothpick to the opposite side of his mouth. "They're my friends as well as my breadwinners. Season's over. I'll be taking them to the valley tomorrow to turn them out for the winter."

Taylor clapped the cowboy on the shoulder. "Nice of you to let us use them today. The boys have been looking forward to it."

"Shoot, man," Quent said, "it's your land we ride

on from spring to fall. The least I can do is let you take a ride whenever you want."

Annie glanced at Taylor. The man still had surprises up his sleeve. He hadn't told her that he owned this land. They were standing at the foot of a beautiful, unspoiled mountain at the outskirts of Vail.

"Any recommendations?" Taylor asked, gesturing toward the corral.

Quent nodded. "I suggest you take the red roan. He's the lead horse I usually ride. The rest of them are all gentle enough for the kids, so they can take their pick." He ambled to the corral in his loose-hipped gait, and when he entered, the boys looked at him in awe. In no time he'd adjusted all their stirrups, hoisted them into the saddles, and had them lined up. Brian was delighted to be riding directly in front of Annie, who, as an experienced rider, had volunteered to bring up the rear.

They headed out on a narrow path up the steep mountain trail, winding through the aspen groves, past the spruce, occasionally stirring up rabbits and birds. After a half hour of steady climbing, they clustered in a clearing near the summit to gaze down at the spot where they'd started. Below them, Vail looked like a village made of matchboxes. The highway they'd traveled gleamed like a silver ribbon carelessly tossed and forgotten.

"Gosh, this must be what it looks like from heaven!" Brian exclaimed.

Taylor glanced at Annie sitting on the horse next to him while the kids gazed around and pointed out the grass-covered ski trails on Vail Mountain across from them. Without a word he reached across to take her hand and send her a look that told her how this moment would become a special memory for them.

After the horses had rested, they hit the trail again, climbing higher and winding around to the back of the mountain. Here there were few signs of civilization.

They stopped at a creek sheltered by trees, where the water ran cold year-round. Taylor pointed upstream some twenty yards to a waterfall.

"When the Ute Indians lived here," he said, "they wisely chose to hang the deer and other game they harvested above a waterfall like that one because the meat would stay cool for a long time and not spoil."

Annie watched the boys of Indian descent. As Taylor explained to them the self-reliant ways of their people, they seemed to sit a little straighter on their saddles. Her heart swelled, too, as she realized that Taylor was restoring their self-esteem while he fostered their pride in their heritage. He seemed to know how important it was for these kids without parents to feel good about themselves.

He told them how their forefathers had built their winter lodges to withstand the heavy snowfalls until spring. He explained to them the Utes' reverence for wildlife by telling them how the Indians had thanked the fish and animals for feeding them before they consumed them as food.

He didn't have to tell them that the Utes had been removed from their land, which had covered much of the Colorado Rockies, and moved to southern Colorado and Utah. They already knew that, and for this reason and others, they suffered a sense of rootlessness and abandonment.

They crossed the stream in single file and rode into an empty camp that held a few deserted shacks.

"Who lives here?" one of the boys asked as they gathered up in a group.

"You'll see if we all stay quiet," Taylor replied.

They fell silent, glancing around sharply. Soon a few furry heads popped out of the ground, followed by a few more. The curious, stocky creatures came out of their dens to stand on their hindlegs and gaze at the strangers. Each was about two and a half feet tall, with a long bushy tail.

"What are they, Taylor?" Brian's friend Billy asked.

"Marmots. They're in the woodchuck family. Now, don't dismount," Taylor cautioned the boys, "or they'll run back inside their burrows. They're brave because all summer and fall the trail rides have stopped here. Since the riders never dismounted or disturbed them, the marmots assume it won't happen now. It has taken a while," he explained, his eyes meeting Annie's as he continued, "but they've finally given us their trust."

The marmots grew bolder and advanced a few steps to sit up on their haunches and gaze curiously at the boys, who were still eyeing them. Chip asked, "Do other animals catch the marmots very often?"

Taylor shook his head reassuringly. "No, these furry little guys have got sharp teeth, and they're just scrappy enough to back off most of their predators. Occasionally an eagle will pick one off, if a marmot forgets to remain alert."

Chip looked up to scan the sky overhead but didn't spot an eagle above the canopy of trees.

"Does anyone use the cabins?" Annie asked, glancing at the three primitive buildings standing in a row.

Taylor nodded. "After the snow flies, Quent runs a snowmobile rental at the foot of the mountain. Some of these trails are marked for snowmobile use. A couple of the fellows stay up here to dispense hot chocolate and make sure everyone stays healthy and safe."

"And the marmots?" she asked with a smile.

"They're deep in their burrows hibernating by then. I can assure you that no one bothers them," he said.

She looked into his eyes, hers shining with admiration for him. He was so good with the boys, so sensitive to their needs, so wise and understanding, that her heart swelled with love for him. At that moment she believed that Taylor McQuaid was truly a man she could depend on, a man who wouldn't cast her aside for another woman after a few steamy months.

Bear was right. This man did not have the same failings as her father. Though he *was* like her father in some ways: He had the looks; he had charisma; he could walk into a room and every woman there would turn her head. But Taylor McQuaid had character, and that made all the difference. She suspected that he was the type who could be loyal if he pledged to be. And besides, she was already hopelessly in love with him.

They rode on until they came to a grassy clearing beside a bubbling stream. Taylor offered to have the picnic there, and the hungry boys quickly agreed. Annie and Taylor unpacked the food and set it out while the boys cooled the horses. Then Taylor supervised them while they watered the horses and tied them nearby, while Annie took pictures.

After a hearty meal the boys wandered over the hill to the stream, where they scampered over the rocks and tried to catch fish with their hands. Taylor helped Annie pack up everything, then he sat down on a log beside her and looped his arm around her.

"God, I've missed you," he said.

"I've been with you all day."

"Not like this you haven't." He kissed her hungrily.

"Easy"—she drew a few inches away—"we're still acting as role models, remember?"

"They can't see us," he whispered, bringing his lips back to hers. "Just once more, please, or I think I'll die."

His eagerness pleased her. She wanted to be in his arms, now and forever.

Brian popped over the hill, and the two sprang apart guiltily. "I caught a frog! Wanna see?" He held out his hand and uncrooked his fingers slightly. They both nodded at the captured creature dutifully.

"You can play with him here," Taylor said, "but when it's time to go, don't you think you ought to release him and let him live in the only place he knows?"

Brian frowned. "Okay, but till then he's mine!" With that he scrambled back over the hill to join the others at the stream.

"That was close," Annie remarked.

Taylor nodded. "Well, there's something we need to discuss anyway."

She sat up straighter. "Oh?"

"I have to go to New Orleans next week for the national car show. I made the commitment months ago, and the arrangements are set."

"How long?" she asked.

"Ten days." He sighed. "I'm staying over for some extra meetings with potential customers from overseas."

"I hope you have a good time," she said sincerely.

"I won't . . . unless you join me." The look in his eyes was plaintive. "I know it's short notice, but do you think you could get away—if not the whole ten days, for part of it anyway?"

"I . . . don't know."

"I took the liberty of checking with the airline, and there's still room on the flight. I'd be happy to take care of that and any other expenses—"

"I don't know, Taylor," she interrupted, as a niggling doubt gnawed at her. "Do you usually take your girlfriends along on your business trips?" It was out before she'd even thought it.

He looked at her in surprise. "What does that mean?"

She looked away and shrugged. "Idle gossip, I suppose."

"Well," he said with more than a trace of irritation in his voice. "I suppose that there have been a few times when I've taken a guest with me out of town. It's not something I do casually—or frequently for that matter. But on occasions where I was involved with someone I really cared for—" He stopped and studied her profile for a moment. "What's wrong, Annie?"

She shrugged and tried to paste on a brave smile, but all the ghosts of old doubts planted by the local gossips had suddenly been resurrected in her mind. "It's nothing, really."

He released a long breath. "I thought we were past all that."

"I thought we were too." She touched his arm. "I'm sorry. I don't know what comes over me sometimes."

"Then you'll come with me?" The look in his eyes was so compelling that she forced herself to glance away.

"I . . . I'd better not."

A silence filled the gap between them. "Mind telling me why?" he asked finally.

"Well, it is short notice, and I have lots of new orders rolling in now. Unlike you, I can't afford assistants to cover for me while I'm gone."

She wanted to throw herself into his arms and tell him that she'd follow him anywhere, to the ends of the earth, if he wanted her to. But there was another part of her, a part linked to her sense of self-preservation, that warned her that she was already in too deep and sinking deeper.

He raked his fingers through his hair, the way he always did when he was angry. "It always comes back to that, doesn't it?" There was a chill in his voice that tore at her heart. "You've always got to point out our differences. My past, my friends, my business—and especially my money—annoy the hell out of you! Why can't you realize—"

He didn't finish his sentence. The kids came bursting over the hill, laughing, poking each other, and wrestling playfully.

The boys chattered on the ride back, but Annie and Taylor were unusually quiet. The youngsters eventually fell asleep in the van, while Annie remained awake, lost in her own lonely thoughts.

Twelve

The next several days at the shop were long and miserable for Annie. She tried to start new projects but had no drive to get them going. She had always been able to pour her passion into her art, until now. Her future in the art world had been the backbone of her dreams for years, but it didn't seem so important anymore.

A hundred times she wished that she had gone to New Orleans with Taylor. She knew that she was closing doors in her life rather than opening them, but she couldn't help thinking that although Taylor McQuaid might not have been born with a silver spoon in his mouth, he could afford one now. He was a self-made man, and he was wealthy by her standards. She and Bear lived a rather Spartan existence. After they split the profits on their sales, there were some months when she was lucky to have grocery money.

How could a girl with no society background and modest means fit into Taylor's world? That question ate at her day and night and had since the beginning. Even if Taylor wanted to make their relationship permanent, how could it work with the vast difference in their lifestyles?

Bear had told her that her reasoning made no sense to him at all, but after their initial conversation he'd remained silent on the subject. It was obvious that she was hurting, and anyone who knew her could see that pushing her only made her dig her heels in and grow more stubborn.

That was why he was still trying to tread lightly around her a week after Taylor McQuaid had left for New Orleans. Annie glanced up as he breezed through the back entrance into their shop.

Bear strode to her work corner and tossed two sacks onto her work table. "For you, dear sister."

"What is it?" She was sitting there, staring into space, feeling too lethargic to move.

"It's a surprise." His voice sounded like he was talking to a child. "You're supposed to rip into them to discover their contents. Then you're supposed to oooh and ahhh over my generosity and thoughtfulness."

She sent him the pointed glare that always meant she didn't need anyone to tell her what to do.

In his brotherly fashion he ignored it, and announced the obvious. "Well, aren't you going to open them?" He followed the baiting by a look of mock injury.

"Oh, all right." She opened the larger one to discover a cheese Danish, her favorite. When she looked up at her brother, her eyes were softer.

Bear believed that food was the cure for most ailments. He usually brought her herbs and health foods to cure colds, but it had evidently seemed that sweet rolls were more appropriate for a broken heart.

"Thanks, Bear."

"Time you started packing away the groceries, you know." He scooped up the sack. "I'll take this upstairs and nuke it for you while I make us some coffee."

She nodded her agreement. It was pointless to argue with him. She knew he'd be poking food at her whether she agreed or not. She couldn't remember when she'd eaten last, and yet she had no appetite.

She heard him tromping upstairs. He hadn't waited for her to open the other sack, which wasn't like him. That aroused her curiosity. She opened it to discover a pack of photos.

She opened it and stared at the first one. Tears flooded her eyes as she saw the image of Brian grinning at her as he watered his buckskin horse. She flipped through them, coming at last to the pictures she'd shot the day Taylor had taken her to his cabin.

They'd slipped through the woods down to the lake, where she'd got some great photos of waterfowl and wildlife. Inspiration for her new projects. Inspiration to fill the new orders that had rolled in after the silent auction. She came to the last picture, and a knot swelled in her throat. It was one she'd taken of Taylor clowning around, flapping his arms to simulate a takeoff, pretending to be one of the ducks she'd been unable to photograph, since they had already flown south for the winter.

South for the winter. She wished she could fly somewhere to be away from every place that served as a daily reminder of Taylor McQuaid.

Bear arrived with a tray of steaming coffee and the hot Danish and the day's mail tucked under his arm. After passing her a mug and the plate of rolls, he handed over the stack of mail.

Annie flipped through the envelopes.

Bear leaned across the table to catch a glimpse. "What do we have there—bills again?"

She nodded absently. "Yes, but several new orders as well. It seems that our shop is finally making a regular profit, and a tidy one at that."

Bear grinned. "Just what you've always wanted."

"Yeah, just what I've always wanted." Her voice was a whisper rather than a shout. What was the matter with her? This was what she'd worked for, starved for, dreamed of. Then why didn't she feel half as elated as Bear was? Why wasn't she dancing around the room? Had Taylor turned everything in her life inside out?

Somehow her heart didn't buy that logic. She knew why she had the blues. Deep down, she still wished she'd gone to New Orleans with Taylor, and that kept her spirits down.

She glanced out the window to see a nippy breeze stirring bits of litter into tiny dust devils in the courtyard outside. The fountain stood idle, its familiar trickle silent now that the nights dipped below freezing. The sun behind an overcast November sky failed to cast a shadow. The view only served to depress her more.

She glanced down and began sorting through the new shipment of catalogs. Her hand paused when she came to a magazine. Her eyes widened as they scanned the title: *Creative Cuisine*. She'd forgotten all about the contest. She and Taylor obviously hadn't won the trip to Paris, but she didn't feel terribly disappointed.

She opened the holiday issue and glanced down the table of contents, then she began flipping pages. She came to the section about the cookoff.

It was thrilling to learn that she and Taylor had won an Honorable Mention award, and it was truly gratifying to see her recipe in print. There was also an accompanying picture.

She leaned back to stare at the photo of Taylor standing with his arm draped around her, smiling into her eyes. Suddenly she could see something in that photo that she hadn't been able to recognize any other time.

The look on his face as he gazed down at her was one of pure enchantment. He was a man in love, and it startled her to discover that he must have been in love with her way back then . . . and all the time since.

Why hadn't she been able to see that before? Had she been so wrapped up in her feelings for him that she'd been blind to his feelings for her? Of course, he'd never told her how he felt, but it wasn't that he hadn't tried.

She thought back on the times when he'd told her that there was something he wanted to say, and she remembered that she'd been afraid to hear it, afraid to face it, so she'd always found a way to distract him or change the subject. Perhaps she'd figured that if she didn't let him tell her his feelings, she wouldn't have to deal with them . . . or their far-reaching implications.

All along, she had been the one afraid to face the future and what it might bring for them. With a sickening horror she faced the fact that she was the one, not he, who had always thrown obstacles in their path. She was punishing him for things he had not even done yet, for things that he might never do.

It disappointed her to realize that she had been a coward, unwilling to give the best man she'd ever met a fair chance because of her own petty fears. What was this doing to Taylor? Her lack of trust had surely been a blow to his pride. Her dream of recognition as an artist had come true, but without Taylor to celebrate it with her, it didn't seem as valuable as it once had. She'd had someone special in her life until she'd mistrusted him, insulted him, and shoved him aside.

She had really messed up this time, and she decided at that moment to do something about it. She tucked the magazine under her arm and headed up to her apartment, striding with a purpose.

She looked at the calendar in her kitchen and counted off the days. Taylor would be back from New Orleans soon. And she had to come up with the perfect plan to tell him what she had to say.

The night before Taylor's return, Annie carefully assembled her disguise. The next morning she arranged for a limo to drop her off at McQuaid's just before closing time at his dealership. She spent the rest of the day making her preparations.

When the driver pulled into the alley, she was waiting on the landing, wearing a formfitting halter dress, a broad-brimmed hat, and large, dark sunglasses. She flagged him down with her lace handkerchief. He pulled to a stop and stepped around to open the car door for her as she carefully negotiated the steps in her high heels.

"Good afternoon. Where to, ma'am?"

"McQuaid's, thank you."

She slipped into the backseat, and he inhaled the trailing scent of expensive French perfume. She rehearsed her plan in her head on the ride to McQuaid's. Like most plans of attack, its success depended upon timing. And a measure of reasonably good acting too.

"Would you like me to wait, ma'am?" As directed, the driver had pulled up in front of the huge showroom windows. He had opened her door and was holding out his hand.

She reached out, wearing her long black gloves,

and placed her hand in his. "That won't be necessary." She let him help her out, then she handed him a folded bill. "Thank you."

He drove away as she approached the double doors. Immediately two salesmen, who witnessed the whole charade, rushed to open the doors for her. By this time word was spreading throughout the offices that there was a real customer in the showroom.

"Why, thank you, gentlemen. How nice of you," Annie said in a sugar-sweet voice.

"May we help you, Miss . . . ?"

"Well," she drawled, "I'm here to buy an automobile . . . today." She did her best imitation of a slow Marilyn Monroe walk across the showroom floor.

The salesmen's eyes were popping as they scurried to catch up with her. "Just tell us what you'd like."

"Well, this might surprise you, boys," her voice lowered seductively, "but I am accustomed to the best."

"Oh, I'm sure of that," said the taller of the two young men.

"Then, by all means, show me. Now I do have it right when I assume that your best will also be your most expensive?"

"Yes, ma'am," said the shorter of the two. "That's generally the way it works."

She brought her hand to her chest, which the dress adequately revealed. "That's been my experience too."

"This little nine-eleven Turbo is nice." They ushered her across the room. "It has everything you could ever want."

Annie leaned closer to read the sticker price. She suddenly went lightheaded. A mere hundred thousand. "Yes, I could be happy driving this model."

Most of the office employees would have been leaving about now, but they had gathered behind the reception counter to watch the show.

"It is lovely, but I wouldn't buy anything . . . without trying it out first, would you?"

"No, ma'am," the two said in unison.

"I'll just get the key," said the taller one, "and Fred here will get the door, and you and I will drive this one right off the showroom floor."

Fred's face fell.

"Oh, boys, I wouldn't want to trouble either one of you."

"It's no trouble, ma'am," Fred said quickly. "I'll get the door."

"Well, if you'll pardon me for saying this, I am accustomed to dealing with the man at the top."

Their ready smiles seemed to slide from their faces.

"I do hope you understand"—she reached out to touch their shoulders—"but I wouldn't consider buying this fine automobile unless the owner personally accompanies me on the test drive. That's just the way I do business."

"Of course, the owner," the taller one replied. "Fred, why don't you find Mr. McQuaid while I get the lady a cup of coffee."

Fred scurried across the room and down the hall.

"How do you take your coffee, ma'am?"

"Coffee?" She shifted her weight to her other hip, a movement that the salesman didn't fail to notice. "It's too late for coffee. I generally drink champagne about this time of day."

The salesman cleared his throat. "Not a good before driving."

" she touched his arm playfully, "you are so n glad you're here to keep me out of

He almost swallowed his tongue. "Yes, ma'am."

Fred rapped smartly on McQuaid's office door.

"Come in," Taylor said gruffly, checking the clock on his desk.

"Mr. McQuaid, I wouldn't be bothering you if it wasn't rather important. We have a customer in the showroom who wants to drive the Turbo."

"Then, by all means, take him for a test drive."

Fred took a deep breath. "The customer is a female—oh what a female—and she's ready to buy, money no object."

"Then what is the problem, Fred?"

"She insists on dealing with the man at the top. She won't buy a car unless you accompany her on the ride."

Glancing at the clock again, Taylor sighed. "Can't someone else take care of this?"

"I'd be happy to volunteer, but she's one of those picky ones, boss, She won't go unless it's with you."

"All right." He shoved his chair back from the desk, reaching for his jacket.

"I guess it goes with the territory, sir. Actually you might not mind the break. The woman has the nicest—"

"Spare me the description," Taylor interrupted. He'd sworn off women, for the time being. "I'll be out in a few minutes."

By the time Taylor walked into the showroom, Annie was behind the wheel warming up the engine. The two salesmen were holding open the double doors.

Taylor's heels clicked across the showroon floor as he approached the car. Sliding into the passenger seat, he closed the door. "Hello, I'm Taylor McQuaid," he said evenly, reaching across to shake hands.

"Buckle up, Mr. McQuaid." Annie released the clutch while pressing the accelerator and burned rubber across the showroom floor. The salesmen, their mouths agape, watched her squeal the tires off the lot.

"Good Lord!" Taylor exclaimed, grasping the armrest for support. His eyes widened as they darted out in traffic.

"Keep your shirt on, McQuaid. I'll slow down." She flipped on the radio. "Nice stereo."

Taylor leaned toward her. "Wait a minute. Have we met? You look familiar."

"Well . . ." With one finger, she pulled her glasses down her nose, batted her eyelashes at him, then shoved the glasses back in place. "You could say if we're not familiar now, we're gonna be."

"Oh, hell, Annie," he groaned. "I should have known it was you. I'm in no mood for games. Turn around."

"Not yet." She took a corner, then sped down a deserted lane. "This is *my* test drive, remember?"

"Okay, then, pull over and let me out."

"You're really mad at me, aren't you?"

"Well, hell, Annie, shouldn't I be? I'm in love with you, and you make it plain I don't stand a chance— now pull over," he ordered as she hit a pothole that threw them both to the ceiling.

"No." She turned off the lane and through an open gate that led into a shaded glen.

A moment later she switched off the engine, extracted the key, tugged at her bodice, and dropped the key down her front.

"I don't know what that proves," he said. "I'm not above going after that key."

She shrugged and got out of the car. Slipping off the high heels, she tossed them onto the seat, and leaned down to look at him through the open window. "I'm counting on it, McQuaid."

She walked into the woods, her hips swaying provocatively.

That did it! Taylor climbed out of the car and slammed the door. What did she think she was doing? This was totally out of character for Annie Malone.

As Taylor strode down the narrow path she'd taken, he spotted her standing in the midst of a beautiful clearing. His eyes widened as he spotted a small round table covered with white cloth. Atop it were silver serving dishes and candles. On either side were small wooden chairs he recognized from Annie's kitchen.

She turned, pulling off the hat and glasses, and held out her arms to him. Despite his intentions to do otherwise, he walked right into them.

"You're driving me crazy, woman. Do you know that?" he growled against her hair.

She smiled up at him. "That's because I love you so much."

The stormy look in his eyes softened. "Say that again." He had to be sure he'd heard her correctly.

"I love you, Taylor McQuaid. And I've done a lot of thinking in the past several days."

He settled her against his hip and looked into her eyes, ready to listen.

"I know now that my fears about you were rooted in my past. I've forgiven my father and taken a long, hard look at the unfairness of my old attitudes. I was carrying around a lot of emotional baggage that I don't want in my life anymore. I don't resent your success, or your money, or your lifestyle, and I'm sorry that I misjudged you. I want a future for us. Do you think you could give us another chance?"

He drew her to him, kissing her with all the

pent-up fervor of too-long denial. This was the love he'd thought he'd lost. This was the woman he wanted more than anything or anyone. These were the words he'd been waiting to hear from her.

"I know it's shameful for me to proposition you, but—"

His eager kisses dispelled any doubts that she might have had about his acceptance. "I want you alone, Annie Malone, for days—maybe weeks," he murmured suggestively when their lips parted moments later. "I'll show you how I feel about your 'proposition.'"

She hugged him fiercely, unable to get close enough, unable to get enough of him. He was the only man she'd ever love, and she'd nearly lost him.

When their lips parted moments later, he smiled into her eyes. "I'm looking for a woman to marry, Annie."

She grinned. "Now, this is a remarkable coincidence Mr. McQuaid. As it happens, I'm in the market for a husband." She wrapped her arms around his neck and kissed him hungrily. When their lips parted, she gazed into his eyes. "Want to team up?"

"You've got yourself a deal, lady."

She lifted her mouth to his again, and they kissed with all the passion they'd denied themselves for days, a passion they had thought would never come again.

"Tell me again," he requested minutes later.

Her eyes were shimmering with joy. "I love you . . . and I will marry you."

"Well," he said with devilish twinkle, "I know where there's a nice honeymoon suite in Vail."

She slanted a teasing glance up at him. "Yeah, and I hear it was wasted the last time a couple was there."

His chuckle sounded deliciously wicked. "I can guarantee it won't be this time. Let's go."

With a wink Annie drew his mouth back to hers. "Of course, darling. We'll be on our way . . . as soon as you find your car key."

THE EDITOR'S CORNER

What a marvelously exciting time we'll have next month, when we celebrate LOVESWEPT's ninth anniversary! It was in May 1983 that the first LOVESWEPTs were published, and here we are, still going strong, still as committed as ever to bringing you only the best in category romances. Several of the authors who wrote books for us that first year have become *New York Times* bestselling authors, and many more are on the verge of achieving that prestigious distinction. We are proud to have played a part in their accomplishments, and we will continue to bring you the stars of today—and tomorrow. Of course, none of this would be possible without you, our readers, so we thank you very much for your continued support and loyalty.

We have plenty of great things in store for you throughout the next twelve months, but for now, let the celebration begin with May's lineup of six absolutely terrific LOVESWEPTs, each with a special anniversary message for you from the authors themselves.

Leading the list is Doris Parmett with **UNFINISHED BUSINESS**, LOVESWEPT #540. And there is definitely unfinished business between Jim Davis and Marybeth Wynston. He lit the fuse of her desire in college but never understood how much she wanted independence. Now, years later, fate plays matchmaker and brings them together once more when his father and her mother start dating. Doris's talent really shines in this delightful tale of love between two couples.

In **CHILD BRIDE**, LOVESWEPT #541, Suzanne Forster creates her toughest, sexiest renegade hero yet. Modern-day bounty hunter Chase Beaudine rides the Wyoming badlands and catches his prey with a lightning whip. He's ready for anything—except Annie Wells, who claims they were wedded to each other five years ago when he was in South America on a rescue mission. To make him believe her, Annie will use the most daring—and passionate—

moves. This story sizzles with Suzanne's brand of stunning sensuality.

Once more Mary Kay McComas serves up a romance filled with emotion and fun—**SWEET DREAMIN' BABY,** LOVESWEPT #542. In the small town where Bryce LaSalle lives, newcomers always arouse curiosity. But when Ellis Johnson arrives, she arouses more than that in him. He tells himself he only wants to protect and care for the beautiful stranger who's obviously in trouble, but he soon finds he can do nothing less than love her forever. With her inimitable style, Mary Kay will have you giggling, sighing, even shedding a tear as you read this sure-to-please romance.

Please give a rousing welcome to newcomer Susan Connell and her first LOVESWEPT, **GLORY GIRL,** #543. In this marvelous novel, Evan Jamieson doesn't realize that his reclusive next-door neighbor for the summer is model Holly Hamilton, the unwilling subject of a racy poster for Glory Girl products. Evan only knows she's a mysterious beauty in hiding, one he's determined to lure out into the open—and into his arms. This love story will bring out the romantic in all of you and have you looking forward to Susan's next LOVESWEPT.

Joyce Anglin, who won a Waldenbooks award for First Time Author in a series, returns to LOVESWEPT with **OLD DEVIL MOON,** #544. Serious, goal-oriented Kendra Davis doesn't know the first thing about having fun, until she goes on her first vacation in years and meets dashing Mac O'Conner. Then there's magic in the air as Mac shows Kendra that life is for the living . . . and lips are made for kissing. But could she believe that he'd want her forever? Welcome back, Joyce!

Rounding the lineup in a big way is **T.S., I LOVE YOU,** LOVESWEPT #545, by Theresa Gladden. This emotionally vivid story captures that indefinable quality that makes a LOVESWEPT romance truly special. Heroine T. S. Winslow never forgot the boy who rescued her when she was a teenage runaway, the boy who was her first love.

Now, sixteen years later, circumstances have brought them together again, but old sorrows have made Logan Hunter vow never to give his heart. Theresa handles this tender story beautifully!

Look for four spectacular books on sale this month from FANFARE. First, **THE GOLDEN BARBARIAN,** by best-selling author Iris Johansen—here at last is the long-awaited historical prequel to the LOVESWEPT romances created by Iris about the dazzling world of Sedikhan. A sweeping novel set against the savage splendor of the desert, this is a stunningly sensual tale of passion and love between a princess and a sheik, two of the "founders" of Sedikhan. *Romantic Times* calls **THE GOLDEN BARBARIAN** ". . . an exciting tale . . . The sizzling tension . . . is the stuff which leaves an indelible mark on the heart." *Rendezvous* described it as ". . . a remarkable story you won't want to miss."

Critically acclaimed author Gloria Goldreich will touch your heart with **MOTHERS,** a powerful, moving portrait of two couples whose lives become intertwined through surrogate motherhood. What an eloquent and poignant tale about family, friendship, love, and the promise of new life.

LUCKY'S LADY, by ever-popular LOVESWEPT author Tami Hoag, is now available in paperback and is a must read! Those of you who fell in love with Remy Doucet in **RESTLESS HEART** will lose your heart once more to his brother, for bad-boy Cajun Lucky Doucet is one rough and rugged man of the bayou. And when he takes elegant Serena Sheridan through a Louisiana swamp to find her grandfather, they generate what *Romantic Times* has described as "enough steam heat to fog up any reader's glasses."

Finally, immensely talented Susan Bowden delivers a thrilling historical romance in **TOUCHED BY THORNS.** When a high-born beauty determined to reclaim her heritage strikes a marriage bargain with a daring Irish soldier, she never expects to succumb to his love, a love that would deny the English crown, and a deadly conspiracy.

And you can get these four terrific books only from FANFARE, where you'll find the best in women's fiction.

Also on sale this month in the Doubleday hardcover edition is **INTIMATE STRANGERS** by Alexandra Thorne. In this gripping contemporary novel, Jade Howard will slip into a flame-colored dress—and awake in another time, in another woman's life, in her home . . . and with her husband. Thoroughly absorbing, absolutely riveting!

Happy reading!

With warmest wishes,

Nita Taublib

Nita Taublib
Associate Publisher
FANFARE and LOVESWEPT